Falling for

P

-A Story

Melikia Gaino

Copyright © 2015 by True Glory Publications
Published by True Glory Publications LLC
Facebook: Melikia Gaino
Join our Mailing list by texting TrueGlory at 95577

Cover Design: Michael Horne
Editor: Kylar Bradshaw

Acknowledgements

Heavenly Father Lord above, I would like to take this time and say thank you for not leaving me nor forsaking me. Thank you for the Faith you have put upon me, Thank you for loving me and continuing Blessing me. Father, I owe everything to you and all I can say is thank you and I love you.

In Jesus Name,

Amen

I would like to start off by saying thank you to the Gaino and Williams/Mabry family for their love and support. Next, I want to say thank you to all of my friends, who encouraged me to become a writer. I would also like to thank you, Shameek Speight and True Glory Publications for giving me the opportunity to showcase my creative stories. Lastly, I would like to all of the readers and fan, I am so appreciative of you all, for the support and motivation. Again, thank you all.

Table of Contents

Falling for a Drug Dealer

Part III

When the shit hit the fan!!!!!

Chapter 1

This is my party: Kim

Kim had the shock of her life. The man that she loved, but hated at the same time had just showed up at her party and revealed the most shocking news she had ever heard. She stood there staring at Shawn as he was talking to Quan with her mouth open. So many thoughts were going through Kim's head as she tried to figure out how they could be brothers.

"Yo! What you mean? I been taking good care of your girl and son?" Quan asked, ready to whip his brother's ass for talking reckless.

"I told your ass this is my woman and my son. You did a good job nigga now step before I make you leave." Shawn said, ready to put a claim on his woman and son. No one was going to get in his way least of all his brother.

"Yo, dawg you been gone for two years. TWO FUCKIN YEARS SHAWN!!" Quan exclaimed. "You don't have anything over this part of town anymore."

While the two argued, the whole party was looking at the action because they were just as confused as a stuck in place Kim. A glance at Shawn showed that he was tired of arguing with his brother. Out of nowhere, he swung and hit him in the jaw. Quan was caught off guard, but immediately swung back, punching Shawn in his left jaw, causing his head to turn. Shawn grabbed Quan by his collar while upper cutting him in the stomach. All hell broke loose and the two brothers started to go at it. Kevin and Moe couldn't sit around and let the kids and

1

other guest see them fight, so they both jumped up and broke them apart. Kevin grabbed Shawn, while Moe grabbed Quan. Shawn was mad to the point that he could have killed Quan, brother or not. Kevin took him from the back yard to the front to talk to him.

"Yo, man where the fuck you been at?" Kevin asked his best friend that he hadn't seen in so long.

"Man fuck that right now. Why the fuck you let Kim go out and start fucking with my brother?" Shawn asked angry at his best friend. He felt like Kevin betrayed him.

"What the fuck, man? You coming at me with that shit. Dawg, you were gone for two motherfucking years yo. I sit around watching that girl go through so much heartache and pain when your ass left her. Did your dumb ass know she almost lost y'all child because she was so sick when you left her 6 fucking months pregnant. Quan came along and made her smile again and made sure that she delivered a healthy baby, something your ass ain't think about when you left her alone. Hold on, how the fuck was I supposed to know that was your brother? Some motherfucking best friend you are." Kevin said pissed off himself now.

Shawn realized that he was wrong on many levels. He knew he hurt his woman, his best friend, brother and could have hurt his son if he already didn't. For the first time in his life, he broke down and let a tear fall from his eye. He looked at Kevin and said "Man, I fucked up. I know she hate me. I can't live knowing that Kim hates me. I really didn't want to hurt her son."

Even though Kevin was mad, he knew he wouldn't be for long. "Tell her everything. Maybe she'll understand. Yo, go

2

talk to her right now and when you finish, we gonna talk about where your ass been at all this time."

Shawn laughed at his nigga. "Aight nigga let me go and get this shit together. One more question?"

"What up fool, with your punk ass?"

"What she do with my house?" Shawn asked, remembering the house him and Kim bought together and they made plans to spend their life in together.

Kevin laughed and said, "Nigga, she still have it. Everything is still in place, I guess she was hoping or had a feeling you would be back because everything is still the same. Only difference is there are no pictures of you in the house. She didn't want to look at you when she was pregnant so she had the girls pack your shit up and put it in the basement."

"Damn, I really fucked her up in the head." Shawn said to Kevin before they walked back to the back yard. This time everyone was trying to figure out what just happened. Shawn looked around and saw Kim with her girls Lisa, London, Loren, Danni, India, Jasmine and Tracey. He walked over there as if he didn't just cause a scene at her birthday party.

"What's up ladies?" He said making eye contact with everyone. Shawn turned to Kim, "Can I talk to you for a minute?" He asked, never takin his eyes off of her. He had to admit he loved her even more since he was face to face with her. Kim looked the exact same way, but more beautiful than before.

Before Kim could say anything India said "No you cannot talk to her after the way you just acted a few minutes ago."

"Girl mind your damn business, and bring your ass over here. Let your friend be a grown woman." Kevin said getting his woman in check. India just looked at Kevin like he was crazy but didn't say a word as she walked over to him.

"Please Kim, just talk to me for 5 minutes. If you don't like what I'm talking about I will leave you alone, I promise. But I have to let you know what is going on and why I did what I had to do." When she looked in his eyes, the pain and happiness both over took her at one time and she began to cry. When Shawn saw the tears fall from her eyes, he kneeled down in front of her and whispered in her ear "I'm sorry for hurting you. You still my cry baby though."

Kim just stood up without saying anything and grabbed Shawn's hand pulling him towards the house. All of her friends were shocked to see her grabbing Shawn's hand. Not only were they shocked but from across the yard Quan was watching the whole thing. He was so pissed off that he wanted to kill Shawn— even if it was his brother.

"Man, did y'all see that shit?" Quan said to his crew. "What the fuck she think she's doing? She going to make me kill somebody".

"Man, just calm down. You know Kim love you and she ain't going to do nothing stupid." BJ said to keep his friend calm.

"I hope so." He replied as he passed the jay to Terrence.

Meanwhile, Kim led Shawn up the stairs to her and Quan's room. When they got to the room Kim sat on the bed, twisting her hands in front of her. They were silent for 2minutes but it felt like hours. Shawn knew he had to break the silence first.

"You look great Kim."

"Thanks, but let's cut to the chase. I know you ain't just show up on my birthday to tell me that I look great. Where the fuck you been at?" Kim asked staring him in the eyes.

"Well, I came back to get my woman and son."

Before Shawn could finish Kim interrupted him with a cock of her eyebrow at his statement, "Woman? Son? I don't think you have neither here in this house."

"Yo, stop playing." Shawn said not liking the fact that Kim was playing him.

"I'm not playing. If you had a woman or child here you wouldn't never left them all alone for two years. If I didn't love my son to death, I would have said I should have listened to my brother. No fuck that, I should have which mean I would have never met a sorry piece of shit like you." Kim said balling her hands into fists.

"Yo, Kim I'm already going through a lot right now. Please don't treat me like this. I told you I wanted to talk so I can let you know what was going on with me." He said, feeling so bad because he can hear and feel the hurt in Kim's voice.

"I'm listening." She said. She wanted to hear what excuses he could come up with. Why after missing for 2 years, walking out and leaving her on her own, did he come back?

"I had to leave you. It was the only way you could be safe. You know what I did for a living and it was a leak in our operation. The only way to make sure you and our son were safe was for me to leave and handle that. I had to do what I had to do.

5

You know what I mean?" Shawn was explaining but Kim didn't get what that had to do with leaving her.

"So why did you have to leave me. How was that protecting me?" Kim asked.

"I had to put in work ma. I didn't want anything to link back to you and my seed. So to protect you I had to leave you. If someone was looking for me, they would have came after you. So I had to get you out of the equation because if they looking for someone they would go after the ones they love."

"So, you telling me you were in New York this whole time?" She asked with a questioning look, squinting her eyes.

Shawn stuffed his hands in his pockets, while leaning against the dresser. "Naw, ma I was in Spain. It took me two years to get my shit together."

Looking at him, she was at a loss for words. Some shit wasn't adding up to her. Suddenly not feeling like talking anymore, Kim stood up and walked over to the door, opening it. "You have to leave now." She said calmly.

Shawn looked at her as if she lost her mind. "What?"

"I'm sorry Shawn. I understand you had to protect me the only way you knew how but I would have taken that chance with you, and right now I'm not ready for you to be back in my life or my son's. So you have to leave."

"You know what ma, all I can do is respect your wishes and leave but I do love you and you know you still love me." Shawn stoop up and was about to walk out the door and said "By the way, Happy Birthday Kim" and gave her a little box. When Shawn disappeared from view, she opened the box to find a beautiful gold ring nestled inside. Beyond shocked, she knew exactly what that ring meant and knew the real reason Shawn came back on that day. He was going to propose to her.

Chapter 2

India

"Can you believe that Shawn and Quan are brothers?" India asked on their way to home from the party.

Kevin was focused on the road and answered India dryly "Naw, I can't believe it"

India picked up on his dryness. She turned in her seat to him. "What the fuck is your problem?"

He shook his head and shrugged. "Ain't no problem ma. I'm just tired."

"Yeah, whatever. Any way how you going to try and play me in front of my people today?" India asked not forgetting what Kevin said to her.

"Yo, I ain't play you. You should just shut up and let my man talk to his woman." Kevin said keeping his eyes on the road.

"I don't know who the fuck you talking to. First, if he was your man you would have knew where he was at for two years. Second, if Kim was his woman he would have been there for her." India said raising her voice to get her point across.

"Man, calm down before you wake up the twins. And plus you don't know what the fuck is going on between Kim and Shawn, so you need to stay out of it." Kevin said looking in the mirror making sure that the twins were still sleep. He was trying not to fuss because he didn't want her to blow his high and she was on the verge of doing that. India didn't feel like fussing either. She just wanted to protect her friend from getting hurt

8

again. She turned to look out the window, letting the radio be the only noise in the car.

Once they pulled up in their drive way, Kevin's phone started to go off as it was on cue. He read the text message and put the truck in park. He went to the back door and had one child in each arm, while India went and opened the door for him. Going straight upstairs and putting the kid's night clothes on, he made sure they were tucked in. Once he walked out of the kids' room, he looked down the hall and watched India undress. Kevin had to catch his self from getting hard and get it under control before he end up in the room fucking the shit out of India.

"Yo, ma I'm out." Kevin yelled down the hall.

India came in the hallway fully exposed, leaning a hip against the opened door. "Where are going this time of night?"

"I'm going out. I'll be back later." Kevin said before running out the door.

Before India could open her mouth to curse him out, he was gone. She was so pissed that she stormed off to the shower. She took the longest shower possible to try and calm herself down. She and Kevin hadn't had sex in awhile and she thought tonight would be a good night. When she got out of the shower she was still pissed off. All she could do was sit on the bed and remember when she wasn't committed to anybody and how she used to have so much fun. She missed those days. She wanted to check on her friend and also be nosy about what she and Shawn were talking about so she picked up the phone on the nightstand and called Kim. The phone rang 3 times before her sister Angel answered, popping gum.

"Hello?"

"Lil girl put your sister on the phone." India said.

"What you want with my sister with your nosey ass." Angel asked.

"When I see you Angel, I'm going to fuck you up." India threatened her as she always does.

"Yeah sure you are." She said before taking the phone to Kim.

"Hello" Kim said once she got the phone.

"Yo, Kim I'm going to fuck Angel up one of these days." India informed Kim.

She chuckled. "Not if I don't do it first. Any who what's up with you? I just saw you less than an hour ago. I thought you and Mr. Man was going to be busy all night long. Remember you told us don't call you tonight." Kim said laughing. India told, more like yelled at her friends, to not call her all night cause she would be fucking Kevin.

"Well, I see everybody in that house has jokes today. Any way that Nigga just left, didn't let me know where he went or nothing. Got a fucking text and was like I'm out. Now y'all see why I hate being in relationships." India said kind of venting on the phone to Kim.

"Yeah, I feel you. Quan has been acting different ever since Shawn showed up today. After the party he hardly said two words to me, and then he told me he was going out because he needs to clear his mind."

"What did you and Shawn talk about when you lead him in the house?" India asked, wanting to know the details on what happened.

"I knew it was a catch to why your ass called me. You already knew I was going to tell you what we talked about but I had to get my thoughts together. Anyway, he told me the reason why he left, where he was at, why I couldn't know about none of this and he was going to propose to me on my birthday."

"What!" India yelled through the phone. "He was going to do what? That nigga thinks he can leave for 2 almost 3 years and can just show up with a ring and think you should just up and take him back?" She asked.

"I guess. I told him I don't want him around me or my son. He doesn't have any family on this end."

"How did he know where you live now?" India also wanted to know that small detail.

"He went by his mother's house before he came over. He asked his mom do she see Xavier and she informed him she do and showed a picture of him. Then he asked where I stayed because he wanted to see him and make things right with me. So, she gave him the address."

"Now, I understand how he knew what X look like and where you live." India said putting pieces together.

"Yeah, because I was confused on how he knew about where I stay."

India held the phone to her ear with her shoulder as she turned the TV on. "So what did he say about his house?"

11

"Nothing… I ain't give him a chance to say anything about the house before I put him out. I think Kevin already told him about the house anyway."

"What's make you think that?" India asked.

"Think about it. Shawn is his best friend and I know Shawn. That is something he asked Kevin."

"True, I know he told him." India agreed. They talked for an hour then Kim told India she was going to call it a night.

India was flipping channels when she started to doze off. She was woken up by the phone ringing. Half sleep she answered it groggily.

"Hello."

"I know your ass is not in the bed." Peaches said loud.

India pulled the phone away from her ear. "Hell yeah I was sleep. I have been up early helping Kim with her party. What's up? I know it's a reason you calling me this late." She asked still half sleep.

"Well, miss grumpy I was calling to let you know that my cousin in law is at the club freaking mad girls." Peaches said.

"What? What club? Who he with? What girls?" India asked, sitting up, wide awake now.

"He at the club *Passion* with Kim baby daddy, and I have no idea who the bitches is." Peaches answered her cousin.

"Thanks cuz, I'm going to handle this. Thanks for looking out." India said, trying to hide the hurt from her cousin.

"No problem cuz, anytime." She said getting off the phone with India.

India called and called Kevin phone over and over and he didn't answer not once. That just made her angrier. She wanted to get him back. Play him at his own game.

Chapter 3

London

London woke up to the sound of cartoons playing in her ear. She already knew who it was with the cartoons so loud.

"Bryant cut that TV down." She said not even looking from under the covers.

Bryant kept the TV up as if he didn't hear his mother talking to him. So, BJ who was also sleep looked at his son who was on the foot of the bed watching TV and said "Bryant I know you hear your mother talking to you. So turn it down now."

Bryant didn't hesitate he turned it down quick.

London got out of the bed and went to her bathroom. She brushed her teeth, washed her face. She came out of the bathroom; and asked her son what he wanted to eat for breakfast. Bryant replied while still looking at the TV. London shook her head with a smile and proceeded to walk downstairs and start cooking.

While she was cooking for her men, BJ walked up behind her and pulled her against his chest.

"Can you let me go Brandon before our food burn?" London said, loving the feeling of BJ against her too much.

"Oh so now you want me to let you go, and you putting the government out there too." BJ said before letting her go so she can finish cooking. He loved to watch London cook so he hopped on the island counter and watched her do what she do at the stove. When she was done cooking, BJ was staring at her ass. She turned around and caught him.

14

"What are you looking at Brandon?" London asked already knowing the answer.

"I was looking at that ass of yours." He said never shy and speaking what's on his mind.

"You a mess boy." That was the only thing that London could come back with.

"I know. Come here I need to ask you something." BJ said telling her to walk over to him with his finger.

"You can tell me while I'm over here." London said not trying to get close to BJ. She knew that if she got within his reach, they wouldn't be eating till later.

"What you scared of? Come here woman." BJ said a little more forcefully.

London walked over to him slowly. When she was close enough to him, he grabbed her wrist and pulled her into him. He grabbed her face softly and started to kiss her passionately, slipping his tongue inside her mouth. He moved his left hand from her face, down her flat stomach to her ass, giving it a squeeze. London moaned into the kiss, reaching up to grab BJ's shorts. They were about go further until Bryant came in the kitchen.

"Mommy, daddy?" Bryant said looking up at them.

BJ and London sprung apart as if they had been caught by their own parents.

"Go to the table lil man." London said, fixing her clothes.

"Yeah you lil cock blocker." BJ said hopping off the counter following his son to the table after slapping London on the ass.

London gave both of them their plate and joined them at the table. They ate their food, and then BJ looked over at London and asked "When are we going to make another one?"

The question caught London off of guard and she almost choked on her food. "Another one of what?" She asked, still trying to clear her throat.

BJ looked at her as if she was crazy for asking that question. "Let's make another baby London." He said slowly, breaking it down so she can understand him.

"Oh, I have to think about it." She said in a joking tone but in her mind she was very serious. After having Bryant she been shying away from sex and making sure they strapped up. She wasn't ready for another baby yet and possibly ever.

"So, lil BJ you want a brother or sister?" BJ asked his son who he knew would be on his side.

"Yes. I want a brother." Bryant said excited, looking between his mom and dad.

London just sat back and watched them. She knew it was self-fish but she wasn't ready to increase their family yet. She grabbed the plates off the table and took them to the kitchen to get away for a few. While she cleaned up the kitchen and did the dishes, BJ got Bryant dressed so they can go hang out together. By the time London was done cleaning up, both of the men were dressed and ready to leave out. They gave London a kiss and headed out the door. As soon as they left, London got dressed and headed out the door so she can meet up with her girls.

Chapter 4

The Meet Up

It was that time again for the girls to have the meet up. It been a week since Kim party and they all had things to talk about. They wanted something cheap and fast so they decided to go to Red Lobster. The time to meet up was 4pm, which gave everyone time to find a baby sitter if need be. Shockingly this time for their met up Danni was the first to arrive. Then the other girls followed behind. They were happy to see each other as always. When they got together they always acted as if they just didn't see each other a couple of days ago or just talked on the phone. They exchanged hugs and went to take their seats.

As the waiter came to take their orders, it was time for them to be a show because the waiter was young and fine. He had neatly twist dreads, nice brown skin that looked so smooth and a smile that would make you have a tsunami. After he took their drink orders he brought their biscuits. So, while they waited for Mr. sexy to bring their drinks back out. Lisa started the conversation.

"So, ladies what's been up with y'all?" Lisa asked to no one in particular. Everyone was quiet for a minute trying to think what they were going to share to their friends.

"Well, me and Zoe are doing good. The only thing is I want him to stop this damn hustling, because I'm not doing any more time with him. That is a promise." Tracey said, sitting there venting to her friends till the waiter came back and took their order. Once he left, Tracey looked at the rest of her friends, wanting to know what was going on in their lives. "Now, I know I'm not the only one with problems in the house hold."

India cleared her throat so she could get ready to let her friends know what was going on in her life.

"Y'all know how me and Kevin are. We don't give a fuck about where or when we fuck, but lately he hasn't even touched me. I would make suggestions about sex and he would change the subject. We promise to stop clubbing so much and I been getting word that this nigga been at mad clubs and shit. I don't even want to be in a relationship anymore. I miss my old life, having sex, clubbing, drinking, and coming and going when I please. Now, I got motherfucking twins and a dumb ass baby daddy that I am getting tired of. Now, I'm starting to turn to a got damn house wife with no motherfucking ring." She started to fake cry, while looking at her friends. "OMG! I'm turning into y'all boring asses."

London looked around and said, "Well, I guess it's my go, since we are going in order. My life, my life well I have a sex crazed boyfriend which is not a bad thing considering what India going through." London said looking at India. India gave her the finger and smirked.

London laughed a little then continue filling her girls in. "Anyway I notice what BJ been doing and he think he is slick. Lately when we have sex he tries and go raw more and come in me. Today he had the audacity to ask at the table when we are going to make another baby. To be honest ladies I'm not mentally prepared for another baby."

London just stopped talking, letting everyone know that she was done and she was in deep thought.

Everyone took that as a cue to keep going "Well, I don't have any problems. My man calmed down a lot and he is taking

19

good care of our children." Lorren said excited. At the same time she comforted her sister who looked a little out of it.

Danni was busy texting Moe when it came to her turn. Tracey looked over at her and said "Damn bitch, get off that nigga dick."

Danni looked up from the phone and said "Fuck you bitch, and get on some dick."

Everyone at the table laughed. While they were busy laughing, the sexy waiter came back over with their food. Once he walked away from the table, Danni began to update her friends.

None of her friends knew she had something to do with Bryon death, so she would always keep that secret to herself even though lately her past started to come back to haunt her. "Well ladies, yesterday I got a call from Bryon mom and she told me that he was found dead. She asked me a lot of questions to see if I knew what happened or anything. She never knew that Bryon and I had broken up. So I told her I haven't seen or talked to Byron in almost three years after he hospitalized me."

"Damn what she says after she found out that he was whopping your ass?" India asked, intrigued.

"She was shocked. She said she don't know where he got that from and why would he do something like that. She apologized and asked me if I would come to the funeral."

"So is your ass going or nah?" Tracey asked.

"Yeah, just because I liked his mother. So, that's what's going on in my life." Danni said digging into her shrimp scampi and mashed potatoes.

Everyone but Kim had shared. Everyone noticed something wasn't right because Kim didn't touch her food or drink. She just sat there looking dazed out.

"Earth to Kim." Danni said, snapping her fingers in front of her face.

"What?" Kim said when she noticed that everyone was looking at her.

"Bitch you been sitting over there looking out of it the whole damn day. What the fuck is wrong with you?" Tracey asked.

"Ain't anything wrong with me. I got a lot on my mind right now." Kim said shrugging her shoulders.

"Are you going to share what is on your mind?" Lisa asked, leaning a hand on her forearm.

"I don't want to. I'm cool." Kim said nonchalantly.

"Well, I have a question to you Kim. How in the hell are you going to date a dude and his brother?" Lorren asked.

Kim just looked at Lorren and rolled her eyes. "First they have the same father, they don't talk about each other and they never were seen together. They are more like business partners than brothers. When they met up they were secretive with it. Anymore questions?"

"Yeah, what is going on in that head of yours?" Lisa said, leaning her head to the left.

Kim took a sip of her drink and prepared to inform her friends what she was going through. "Well ever since Shawn showed up Quan been acting weird. He been distancing himself from me and that night of my party he asked me "Did I fuck Shawn in our room, when I went in the house with him?" that man has gone crazy."

"Not only that, Shawn call all the time asking dumb questions, "what you do with my house, where my cars, my clothes?" He is getting on my nerves and every time he calls Quan gets more pissed off." Kim said.

"So you ain't give that man back his shit yet?" London asked smiling.

"No, I feel he don't deserve it. I would give it to him in due time." Kim said shrugging her shoulders.

"Where he been staying?" Danni asked.

"I don't know, maybe his mother's house. I don't care where he been at." Kim said still showing some hurt.

"Kim, you still love Shawn don't you?" Lisa asked sensing the pain he caused her.

"To be honest, I really don't know if I love him or not." Kim said quietly.

After the girls went around the table and spoke their peace, they ate their food. When they were done, they sat and brainstormed as to where they wanted to go next. India wanted to go out to the club because she hadn't been out in a long time. "Yo, let's go to the club. I'm trynna party and shit. I'm starting to feel like an old hag."

"I can't go out tonight. Ma is watching X and I know he probably getting on her damn nerves by now." Kim stated.

22

"I'm tired I don't want to go out." Tracey said.

Everyone declined to go out with India one by one. "Man, fuck y'all. Y'all don't ever want to go out anymore." India was mad because she was actually looking forward to going out somewhere and shaking her ass.

Kim felt bad and could tell that India wanted to go out. "India how about we go out Friday? That would give me enough time to inform Quan that he needs to watch X."

"Ok cool. So nobody else is going Friday?" India asked her friends.

Everyone else declined. So Kim and India planned on going to the club Friday.

Chapter 5

Lorren

When Lorren returned home from having a great evening with her friends, she walked into a quiet house. Walking through the house, she wondered where everyone was. She went to the living room then heard the TV on in the movie room. She peeked in the room and saw her children sleep and Rico on the phone.

When Rico noticed her in the door way he hung up his phone. "What up ma? You had fun with your girls?" Rico asked.

Lorren gave him a quizzical look before answering. "Yeah, I had fun. Why you hang up your phone so fast when you noticed me at the door?"

"No reason, I was about to hang up anyway. Why you ask that?"

"I don't know. Lately, you have been very secretive and it's weird."

Rico just looked at her as if she was crazy. "Ma, you know what I do and I been the same way. I don't know what you been tripping on."

Lorren just looked at Rico, and changed the subject. "So how were the kids?"

"You know they are bad as hell. Sike, naw, we had a good time together. Matter of fact it's time to put them in bed, you know I have to hit the streets up in a few." Rico said getting up and picking RJ up.

Lorren followed him with Lacey in her arms. She put Lacey in her bed while Rico put RJ in his. After they put the children to bed, Lorren knew she didn't have long until Rico would go and hustle all night.

"Rico, I want some dick." Lorren said. She and Rico were blunt about everything in their relationship.

"Damn ma, just like that huh? How do I know you want some?" Rico asked playing a game with her.

"You know I'm ready because I said it." Lorren said getting his drift.

"You might say you want it but you ain't showing me that you want this." Rico said. While licking his lips and winking at her.

Lorren began to walk slowly over to Rico. He sat down on the bed as I watched her with lust in his eyes.

Lorren dropped down to her knees and unbuckled Rico's pants. Pulling his dick out from his boxers, she kissed his tip lightly, seeing as he was already hard. She sucked the head into her mouth before using her right hand to hold on to his base. Stroking him from the base, she let her mouth meet her hand while she took more of him into her mouth. She was sucking Rico's dick so good that he had to stop himself from coming in her mouth. He pulled her up and started to kiss her and suck on her neck. He knew what she liked and wanted. He turned her around while pulling her pants and underwear down. Lorren made quick work of her shirt and began to take her bra off. Rico stood to his full height while backing her up to lie down on the bed. Spreading her legs, he kissed her inner thighs while making his way to her pussy. Before Lorren could catch her next breath,

Rico sucked her clit into his mouth and swirled his tongue around it.

"Shit Rico! Babe, put it in." Lorren begged while Rico was between her legs giving her his famous head. He acted like he didn't hear her and continued eating her out. Arching her back, Lorren yelled out that she was cumming. Rico knew it was his time to take full control of the situation. Making his way up her body, he kissed her fully on the mouth, while kicking his pants off. Easing Lorren's legs open further, he pressed the head of his dick at her entrance. He looked down at her to watch her face as he pushed in a little bit.

"Stop playing babe. Put it all the way in." Lorren begged again wanting the whole thing.

Rico rammed his hard dick in her to the hilt. He went so deep that Lorren was still and couldn't move, her eyes wide opened. He was giving her deep and long strokes. They were so caught up into each other, that they didn't notice they were having sex without a condom again. When Lorren realized that Rico didn't have a condom on, she snapped out of the trance.

"Pull out when you about to cum baby." Lorren moaned, loving the feeling of Rico between her legs.

Rico kept stroking inside her, hitting all her spots. "Did you hear me?" Lorren asked while digging her nails in his back. She wasn't ready to have another baby just yet.

"Damn babe I heard you, get your nails. You are messing up my concentration." Rico said, grabbing her hands and pulling them above her head. "Fuck, you feel so good Lorren." He whispered, while kissing her. Lorren's legs started to tremble as she started cumming again, keeping a firm grip on

Rico's dick. "Shit babe." After that left Rico mouth, he pulled out and came on Lorren's stomach. They laid on the bed, out of breath and eyes closed. Lorren was the first to get up and get in the shower after she pulled herself together. When she got out and entered the bedroom, Rico did the same thing he did earlier— hung up the phone when she walked in.

"So who were you talking to on the phone?" Lorren asked Rico.

"It was no one Lorren." He said, while getting off the bed, heading to the bathroom.

Rico was in the shower when his cell phone rang again. Lorren took it upon herself to answer his phone this time. When she picked up the phone, she could hear a woman talking to somebody on her end of the phone.

"Hello?" Lorren asked.

When she got no response, she said hello again. The caller finally realized that it wasn't Rico on the phone she hung up. Lorren was pissed because the number was unknown and she wanted to know why some bitch was calling her man. She got dressed and waited for Rico to come out the bathroom.

As soon as Rico came from out the bathroom with a towel wrapped around him, she launched his phone at his head.

Rico was caught off of guard and almost forgot that Lorren was his woman. He was so mad that he wanted to beat the shit out of her. "What the fuck you do that for?"

"You lying son of bitch. Are you cheating on me?" She asked furiously.

"Ain't nobody cheating on your dumb ass. I should fuck you up." He said looking in the mirror making sure he didn't have a bruise on his forehead.

"You ain't going to do shit. Who was the bitch that called your phone?" She yelled, standing with her arms crossed.

"What are you talking about?" Rico asked with a frown.

"I answered your phone and when the bitch realized it was me she hung up. I should just fuck your face up, you fake pretty ass nigga." Lorren was mad as shit. She was getting angrier because Rico was acting like he didn't know what she was talking about.

"First, why did you answer my phone? Second, you not are going to do shit Lorren. Third, I am the sexiest Nigga you ever dreamed of." Rico said not paying attention to Lorren threats and making jokes out of the situation. He just continued to get dressed so he can leave.

"You always on joke time, but let a nigga call my phone. You would be all up in your feelings."

Rico was fully dressed now, looking at his self in the mirror. "Yo, ma. Imma need you to do my hair. I can't keep wearing these pony tails."

"I'm not doing shit. Ask your bitch who called you to do your hair." Lorren said rolling her eyes at him.

Rico said something in Spanish under his breath. Then he walked over to Lorren. "I love you. I will be back in the morning." He kissed her on the forehead.

"Yeah whatever. If you loved me you wouldn't be fucking other bitches." Lorren said as he walked out the door. Lorren was pissed off that she wanted to just fuck him up.

She went to bed angry that night.

Chapter 6

Danni

Danni sat on the edge of her bed trying to get herself together to make it to her ex-boyfriend's funeral. She didn't want to go because she knows the reason he is dead is because of her. She didn't want it to get linked back to her at all. While Danni stared in space, with her stocking half on and off, Moe came out the bathroom to get her attention.

"Yo, Danni what's wrong with you baby? You have been like that ever since that nigga mother called you." Moe asked.

"I'm kind of scared. What if they find out that I killed him? I don't know how I'm just going to be around his mother as if I had nothing to do with it."

"Trust me, I would take the heat for you if anybody comes towards you. There is no link to us baby. Trust me." Danni and Moe were in deep conversation when Genesis their son walked in the room.

Danni looked at her son, who just woke up. She stretched out her arms to him. "Hey man, come here." He walked over to his mother and Danni picked him up. "Are you ready to go stay over your auntie Staci house?"

"Yes." Genesis said while yawning.

Danni got up and took Genesis in the bathroom so that she could get him ready to go to her sister house.

After all three of them were ready, Moe dropped Genesis off and took Danni to the funeral. He was going to handle business while she was at the funeral and Genesis was staying over Staci house for a couple of days.

Danni noticed as she walked in that the funeral was packed. All of Bryon's family and friends were there. His mom asked Danni to sit on the first row with her. Since he was missing for two years, he had to have a closed casket. The preacher giving the sermon was good, but Danni couldn't focus. All she could do was stare at the picture sitting on top of the casket. In her mind she could hear him say *Danielle I'm sorry* and then the gun going off. That day played over and over in her head while the preacher talked. She was starting to feel very weak and bad for what she did, till she remembered her miscarriage, him beating her and she was put in the hospital. While she was in the middle of her thoughts, Bryon mom squeezed her hand to get her attention.

"Yes?" Danni asked.

"Would you like to say something?" Bryon mom asked her when it was time for people to speak about Bryon.

"No thank you. I don't think it would be a great idea." Danni said.

"Please just pay your last respects honey. This is the closure you need and I know he did a lot of hurtful things to you but you have to get it off your chest."

Bryon's mother gave her confidence. She stood up and walked slowly to the podium. They introduced her as his fiancée. She was nervous as she stood up in front of everyone. She didn't know what she was going to say.

"I'm Danielle. I was dating Bryon for almost five years. I went through a lot with Bryon. It was more downs than ups. I didn't want to get up here today because I can't really say anything nice about him. I know the only way I can have peace with myself is if I let you all know how I feel, and let him know that I forgive him. The last time I saw Bryon, I was in the hospital because he had beaten me that bad. If I would have stayed in my bed one more day, I probably would have been dead today. But, I got up here today first to tell Bryon I'm sorry, and also that I forgive him for everything he put me through. Thank you all for listening to me." Danni said her peace and went to sit back down next to Bryon mother.

While people were paying their respects, Danni texted Moe to let him know that she was ready to be picked up from the funeral. He was busy while out with Terence, so he asked him if he could ask Lisa to pick Danni up.

By time the funeral was over, Lisa was outside waiting for Danni. She gave Byron's mom a hug and hopped in Lisa car.

"What up bitch? How was the funeral?" Lisa asked, pulling out the parking lot.

"Girl it was a show. His mom wanted me to get up there and speak. Girl I told them how it was." Danni replied, gazing out the window.

"So, are you about to go home or you about to go to the mall with me?" Lisa asked.

"Naw girl, I'm going to pass. I want to go home and rest. My lil rugrat is gone. So I'm about to give my bed some ass and my pillow some head." She said, closing her eyes.

32

Lisa dropped Danni off and headed to the mall. As soon as she got in the house, she put on some shorts and a tank top. She headed back down stairs and laid on the couch with some chips and juice and watched a movie. She was so into the movie she didn't notice that Moe walked in the house.

"What you watching?" Moe asked walking over to her and climbing over her.

"I'm watching Taken. This is a good movie."

"I see, you ain't even pay attention when I came in the house." Moe said starting to rub on Danni's body.

"Boy stop, I'm trying to watch the movie."

"I'm trying to get some of them cookies, but you holding out on a nigga." Moe said, rubbing her hips.

"Boy you silly." She said, still watching the TV. Moe started to bite on Danni neck, while rubbing her nipples through her top. She tried to not pay him any attention, but Moe wasn't going to let her get off that easily. He placed his hand inside her shorts. Using his middle finger, he spread her lips apart and pushed his finger into her. Moe started to massage her clit with his thumb, Danni forgot all about the movie that she was watching. She was moaning while trying to hold onto his hand in her shorts. Kissing the side of her neck, he picked up his pace and added another finger to her pussy.

Danni arched back into Moe, reaching back and grabbing his dick through his pants. She began try and unbuckle his pants. "Babe, I need you."

"Shhh, I know babe." He said, taking his fingers out of her wetness and sucking on them.

Still in the spooning position, Moe yanked Danni's shorts down while unbuckling his pants. He pulled her leg up and grabbed his dick to position it at her entrance. Rubbing the head up and down her pussy, he pushed inside her in one thrust. Danni loved the way Moe felt inside of her and she wasn't ashamed to let him know.

"Fuckkkkkkkkkk Moe. I fucking love this dick." She said while grabbing the back of his head. After spooning for a few minutes he grabbed Danni and put her on top in the reverse cowgirl position. Smacking her ass and playing with clit, he watched her as she rode him. Biting his lip, Moe knew he had to get the situation back under control before he came too quickly. He pushed up and put Danni into the doggy style position. They were so lost to the world and high on each other that they didn't notice a police officer taking pictures of them.

Chapter 7

Lisa

"Man I'm so tired." Lisa said to herself as she drove from the mall to her mother's house.

She pulled up in front of the house and grabbed TJ's bag which had his toys and clothes in it. She was supposed to drop his clothes off before she went to the mall, but she got sidetracked when she had to pick Danni up.

"Hey ma, how you doing?" Lisa asked after she walked in the house.

"I'm good sweetie." Tonya, Lisa's mother responded.

"So where are my favorite boys at?" Lisa asked realizing that her son and brother weren't anywhere to be found.

"They went to the basketball court. You know that's your brother's life. I think it's some girls up there though."

"It probably is ma. He took TJ so he can get some numbers." she said thinking about how her brother always tries to be a Mack.

While Lisa and her mother talked and laughed in the living room, Larry and TJ walked in the house. TJ recognized his mother's voice and ran to her.

"Mommy." TJ said excitedly.

"What up lil man? Did you have fun with your uncle?" Lisa asked. While standing up giving her brother, who was close to 6'1" tall now, a hug.

"Yes, we got a lot of girlfriends now." TJ said jumping up and down.

"Yo, man you ain't supposed to tell her that." Larry said picking TJ up like he was about to drop him. TJ was laughing so hard while playing with his uncle.

Lisa stayed at her mother's house for another hour, before she gave her son, mother and brother a kiss. Tonya asked Lisa if TJ could stay the week with her and Lisa was delighted to let her mom watch him. Ever since her mom got clean, she and Lisa have been like best friends. They have just a day when they go shopping or to the spa. Lisa knew that Terence would be busy all day so she tried not to worry him. This week the men had an important meeting so everybody was stressed and busy. Since Lisa knew how stressed and busy Terrence would be, she tries to eliminate it by not calling him so much. She sent him a text letting him know that she was on the way home.

Driving she was mentally planning her day out. She wanted to eat the food she got from Olive Garden, then take a hot bath, and read her proposal for work.

When she got home, she sat on her couch and ate her food. She was in heaven while she ate because she had been craving Olive Garden for a long time. As planned Lisa ate her food and ran her bath water. As soon as she began to relax in her nice bubble bath, the phone rang.

"Who the fuck is it?" Lisa asked herself before answering the phone.

"Hello?" Lisa answered.

"Can I speak to Terence?" A female voice asked.

36

The voice caught Lisa off of guard, "Ummm, he isn't here. May I ask who calling and your reason for calling?"

"This is Shermika, and the reason I'm calling is because I'm tired of Terence not talking care of his daughter Terri."

"Daughter? I'm sorry, but I think you have the wrong Terence." Lisa said trying to keep herself calm.

"No, I have the right man Lisa. I know about you and everything. I didn't call to break up your little happy home, but I just want you to let him know what I said." Shermika said in a calm voice.

"I will make sure I tell him." Lisa said even though she wanted to curse her out. She knew it wasn't her fault but it was Terence's.

After getting off the phone, Lisa was so pissed off that she couldn't relax anymore. She walked back and forth, calling Terence phone over and over and each time she received no answer. That just made her angrier, to the point that she threw her phone clear across the room.

Chapter 8

The Important Business Meeting.

"Yo Q, we need to start this meeting. Lisa is blowing up my phone like crazy." Terence asked, looking down at his phone for the 5th time.

"It's like this. You know my secret partner that I do business with is my brother Shawn." Quan began to tell them why they were having a meeting.

"Yo, Q I never understood why you would keep that that's your brother a secret." Moe said.

"Man, it's complicated. Our own mother's didn't know that our father had another child. When we started out, we were 15 and our father made us promise that no one would know about the business. So he made us keep our partnership a secret and we had to meet up every month to talk about our share of the business. Shawn was in charge of getting a crew, and I was too. That's how it was. So, let's get down to business. Yo, BJ what the business end looking like?"

"Well, the money is getting cleaned up good and all the businesses are doing great. But it is some Mexican dude trying to step on our street. I got word from one the people who work in the corner store."

"So, Moe, you keep the heat clean?" Quan asked Moe.

"You know it. Never let anything stop my focus. I got an eye on the Mexicans too." Moe said, letting Quan know he was on his job.

"Yo Terence what's got your focus over there?" Quan asked looking at Terence.

"Man, I don't know if anything wrong with Lisa. She won't stop calling me."

"So what's up with the higher authority? I'm feeling heat." Quan asked.

"Yeah, that's another reason I wanted to have this meeting along with Q. Moe you got heat on you. Got word from our man Slim, he said they think you had something to do with Bryon. So, stay clean cause they watching you and wifey." Terence told him.

"So T, why you haven't been told me this. My wifey and child might be in danger. How many is on me?" Moe ask showing his anger.

"It's only this one pressed ass cop. They don't have any evidence. Slim said he was a friend of Bryon's so he just taking it personal. So you good son." Terence assured him.

"Alright, but I'm going to handle him." Moe said.

"Just do it crisp and clean. We don't need any heat on us." Quan said to Moe.

"You already know it my Nigga." Moe said smirking.

"Yo, next week we were going to have a meeting with my brother and his crew. So, we know who is on our team or not. That's cool with everybody?" Quan asked looking around at his team.

No one protested and the meeting was over. Everyone went their separate ways.

Chapter 9

Tracey

Tracey was leaving the school in which she worked while calling Staci up. She was so happy that it was Friday.

"Girl, I had the worst day at work. Two fights broke out and I had to write a motherfucking report." Tracey vented to Staci.

"Damn girl, you had a rough day." Staci laughed, "What was the report about?"

"About that damn fight, then their damn mother's came up here trying to fight. I'm so glad to get the fuck out of there." Tracey said, holding the cellphone to her ear while getting in her car.

"I hear that. So, what are you doing today?" Staci asked.

"Girl, Zoe and I are taking Handsome to the UniverSoul circus. What you doing today?" Tracey asked.

"Girl, I ain't doing anything today. Waiting for Danni to come and pick Genesis up. I had him for the whole week because Danni was busy."

"I hear that. At least he's a good kid. Anyway girl, I'm about to go. I'm at the daycare." Tracey said pulling up.

"Ok girl, have fun at the circus." Staci said before hanging up.

Tracey went and picked her son up from daycare and as always she got a bad report about how he was acting. Tracey was mad because she already bought the tickets for the circus. Had she known he was gonna act up like that, she would have just took him home.

Pulling up at her house, she noticed that Zoe was home.

"What up fam?" Zoe asked once they walked in the house.

Tracey was fuming when she faced Zoe. "This damn son of yours got another bad report. I should give them damn tickets away."

"Dag, calm down. I'm going to talk to him and see what he has to say." He said.

Zoe went and had a talk to Handsome because he knew that Tracey was pissed off. After 10 minutes, he came back down stairs.

"Alright Tracey. The reason why he got a bad report was because one of the kids took his toy, and he wanted it back but the teacher thought it was the other kid's. So, he straight for today. He still is going to the circus." Zoe said.

Tracey didn't feel like fussing so she just let it go. When the time turned to 5pm, they left and headed to the circus. When they arrived, there Handsome was so excited. He wanted every toy that was in sight. Being the father that Zoe is, he got Handsome every top he wanted.

Before the show started, Tracey wanted some nachos and Handsome wanted cotton candy and a hot dog. While they were waiting for their food, Tracey heard a familiar voice behind her. When she turned around, she noticed that it was Kenny. When he saw Tracey, he started to smile. He walked over towards her with a cute little boy behind him.

"What's up Tracey?" Kenny said.

"Nothing, I just been chilling. How you been? I see you looking nice. Who is this little man with you?" Tracey said admiring Kenny.

"This is Joel, my son. By the way I have been great and thank you. Who are you here with?" Kenny asked noticing that no one was with her. After they ordered, Handsome had to use to the bathroom so Zoe took him.

Before Tracey could answer, the cashier told her that her food was ready. She grabbed the food and turned her attention back to Kenny.

"Well, I'm here with..." Before she could respond, Zoe and Handsome walked over.

"Oh I see it's finally done, huh babe?" Zoe said, walking up and putting an arm around Tracey's waist.

"Yeah it just got done. Oh by the way babe this is my friend Kenny and his son Joel. Kenny this is Zoe and my son Handsome." Tracey introduced Zoe and Kenny for the first time. This was the first time that they were face to face and you could sense the tension between both of them.

"Oh wow Tracey! You had a son." Kenny stated. He couldn't believe that she had a son by the dude who did her so wrong.

"Yeah, I had a little man. Any who, it was nice to see you again Kenny." Tracey said before the tension could get any stronger.

"Yeah, it was nice to see you again too Tracey. It was nice to meet you Handsome and nice to finally to meet you Zoe." Kenny said, eyeing Tracey from head to toe, making Zoe angrier.

"Yeah it was nice to finally to meet you too." Zoe said not really meaning it. He eyed Kenny liked he wanted to fuck him up.

Zoe and Tracey went their way and Kenny went his. During the whole show, Tracey couldn't stop thinking about how good Kenny looked. She couldn't wait to get home and tell her girls about her run in with Kenny.

Chapter 10

The Club Scene

India couldn't wait till Friday arrived because she was finally going to go to the club. She had dropped the twins off at her parents' house for the weekend. Kim, Peaches, and Jasmine were going to the club with India. She didn't tell Kevin that she was going out, she said she was going to Kim's house and chill with her and X.

All the girls met up at Jasmine's condo which was in downtown D.C. India was so pumped to go to the club that she was ready to leave as soon as she got to Jasmine's house. On the other hand, Kim wasn't as happy because before she left, her and Quan got into an argument. She was so pissed off that when she got to Jasmine's place, she went straight to the bottle and drank. Before they left to go to the club they pre-gamed and made sure they wore revealing outfits. They didn't want to go to their favorite club "Passion" because Jasmine knew she wouldn't be able to do nothing there. They decided to go to one of the new clubs in Silver Spring so they wouldn't run into anyone. When they pulled in front of the club, they noticed that the line was long as shit.

"Yo, I'm not standing in this line" India yelled. She was ready to party but wasn't trying to spend half her night in a line.

"Ay yo Jaz, look who is at the door?" Kim pointed out.

"OMG don't tell me Ace's ass work here." Jaz said excitedly.

"Who the hell is Ace?" Peaches questioned.

45

"Well ladies looks like we about to get in the club for free tonight. Ace is one of the dudes me and Jaz use to hang out with. He went to school with me and when Jaz use to visit we all use to hang." Kim said getting excited to see her child hood friend.

They found a parking spot and walked to the club. They bypassed everyone standing in the line and walked straight to the front where Ace was checking ID's.

Kim leaned over and said into his ear, "Ace. I know you going to hook a sister up."

Ace was caught off guard. He turned around expecting it to be a random girl because he gets that so much. A soon as he noticed that it was Kim, he smiled so hard.

"Kimie with your big head ass and Jazzy Jas what the hell is y'all doing here." Ace said giving them both a hug.

"Trying to get in the club." Jasmine said, smiling.

"I see that smart ass. I see shit ain't change. Y'all know y'all in here." Ace gave them the VIP band and the 21 and over band. He got Kim number and told her he would see her and Jasmine in there.

"Girl, I'm glad you know so many motherfuckers." India said once they got in the club.

"Shut up and get us some drinks." Kim said to India, rolling her eyes.

India walked towards the bar; switching her hips with every step she took. She approached the bar, and there were a few dudes trying to get her attention to buy her a drink. India being India entertained them for the benefit. The men ended up buying her enough drinks for her and the girls. Leaving the bar, India walked back to the group with their drinks. They decided to head over to VIP where they were giving out free drinks. By the time the girls had their third drink, they were ready to hit the dance floor. They were having a good time dancing and enjoying the atmosphere. They left the dance floor for a few minutes to take a couple of shots each. It was an hour before the club let out and Kim was feeling her drinks more than the other girls because of her earlier rage drinking.

The ladies were in the middle of the floor dancing when Kim felt someone grind on her. She began to dance without looking back to see who it was. Then she heard a familiar voice in her ear. She turned around to see Shawn behind her.

"What in the hell are you doing here?" Kim stopped dancing and asked Shawn.

"I'm dancing with my woman." Shawn said looking too good. Kim couldn't stop looking in his hazel eyes. It was turning her on.

"Well, have fun dancing with her." Kim said walking away before she got herself in trouble.

Before she could get off the dance floor, Shawn pulled her close to him. Kim was looking around for her friends who went to the bathroom two minutes before Shawn came over. She needed them to get him away from her before she did something she regrets.

"You know I miss you, Kim. Why you keep running from me?" Shawn said making Kim look at him in his eyes.

"Shawn, I'm not running from you. I don't want to hear that I miss you shit. Plus, I haven't heard from you if a week." Kim said not in the mood for his mess.

"You told me not to call you. I did call you too and your man told me not to call no mo'. So what you want me to do? I swear if that wasn't my brother he would be dead." Shawn said not hiding his anger.

"Well, at least you can ask about your son. Oh! I guess you forgot about him too. You know what Shawn, I'm done with you so let me go. I have to go find my girls." Kim said trying to pull away from him.

"Yo, Kim, why you acting like that. I was going to ask about lil' man. When are you going to leave my brother and come back home with me?" Shawn asked not giving up. Before Kim could answer, the girls walked back over to where she and Shawn were still talking.

"What the fuck you doing here?" India asked showing that she wasn't happy to see Shawn.

He just looked at India then said, "How you doing Miss India? What's up cuz?" He said to Jasmine. "Hey how you doing I'm Shawn and you are?" Shawn introduced his self to Peaches.

"I'm Peaches, India's cousin." She said, looking between everyone in the group.

"Nice to meet you. What you been up to Cuz?" Shawn said to Jasmine.

"So now I'm your cousin again. Whatever Shawn." Jasmine said then walked off to the bar.

"Kim, you ready to go?" India asked knowing that if Shawn was at the club Kevin wasn't too far behind.

"Yeah, my buzz is leaving thanks to somebody." Kim said looking at Shawn. As soon as the girls tried to walk off, Kevin walked up and stopped India.

"What you doing in the club girl?" Kevin questioned India looking at what she had on.

"I'm chilling with my girls. Why you in the club?" India questioned.

"I see you with your girls but this ain't what you told me you would be doing. You already know what I'm doing in the club." He said.

"Whatever nigga I'm grown." India said getting ready to walk away before he blows her high.

"Why the hell you got on that short ass dress?" Kevin asked, not letting her walk away that easily.

"I would see you at home. It's not the time or place for this Kevin." India said, showing that she didn't want to be bothered.

Shawn and Kevin followed the girls to the VIP section where Peaches and Jasmine went to get some last minutes drinks before they left the club.

"Why are you following us?" Kim asked Shawn.

"I need to talk to you Kim."

49

"I don't want to talk to you. I gave you everything you need which means we have no more ties to each other." Kim said waiting for her girls to finish their drink.

"Who drove?" Shawn asked Peaches since she was the only person talking to him.

"Jasmine drove." Peaches said.

Shawn looked over at Kim and grabbed her hand. "Yo, Kim you going with me."

Kim snatched her hand away quickly and looked at Shawn as if he was crazy. "No, I'm not going with you. I have a family at home waiting for me."

Shawn was tired of Kim denying him. All he wanted was to talk to her, so he waited for the girls to leave out of the club and walked them to the car.

"Kim where is your car?" Shawn asked.

"Shawn my car is at my cousin house. What would it take for you to leave me alone?" Kim asked annoyed.

"All I want you to do is go with me. I would take you to get your car and everything." Shawn said.

The only way for Kim to get Shawn off her back was to ride with him. She figured that this would be the final time they talked and she wouldn't have to bug her anymore. "Ok Shawn." Kim said giving in.

While Kim let her girls know that she was going to ride with Shawn, India and Kevin were fussing at each other for being in the club. Kevin decided he was going to follow Jasmine to her house so India could get her car and they both can go home. They both knew they had unfinished business to handle out of the public eye.

Meanwhile in Jasmine's car...

"I hope Kim don't fall for that nigga again." India said thinking that her girl was dumb for riding with him.

"Man, my cousin is smarter than that. She is not going to fall for him." Jasmine said defending Kim.

While the girls talked about Kim in the car, Kim and Shawn were surprisingly having a good conversation. They were in the depth of their conversation her phone rung. Kim looked at it and noticed that it was Quan calling.

"Tell my brother I said what's up?'" Shawn said trying to be funny.

Kim just looked at him and answered her phone. "Hey baby. What's going on?"

"So, where you at?" Quan asked.

"I'm just leaving the club. I'm kind of drunk and I'm going to take a quick nap at Jaz's house to wear the liquor off then I will be home." Kim said not liking the fact that she just lied to her boyfriend.

"Ok babe. Be safe. I'll call and check up on you later. I love you." Quan said.

"I love you too." Kim said before hanging up.

After Kim hung up, she could see the anger on Shawn's face. The remainder of the ride to Jasmine's house was silent.

Chapter 11

India

As soon as India and Kevin walked in the house, the fussing continued.

"Why you had to lie to me India?" Kevin asked, slamming the front door.

"I lied because you always quick to run out to a club or something and when I tell you I want to go out you have to question me." India said pointing at Kevin with her hand on her hip.

"What you need to be in the club for? You got a man and children at home."

"You have a woman and children at home so what's the difference? You met me at a club and you know how I was when you first started talking to me." India was getting pissed off. She turned away from Kevin and headed for the stairs. Dealing with Kevin's hypocritical ass tonight was not on her agenda.

"When I go to the clubs I go to work, not for fun and your ass know that." Kevin said following India upstairs. He was far from done with this conversation.

"Well, last week you must wasn't doing too much work because Peaches saw you freaking at the club."

Waving off India's statement, Kevin kept talking. "Man, I don't want to hear that."

"Right, because you guilty. Are you cheating on me?" India asked, turning around to face Kevin.

"What? What kind of question is that?" Kevin asked, caught off guard.

"We haven't had sex in awhile. I been throwing myself at you and you don't even touch me. When we first started talking I couldn't keep you off of me."

"It ain't anything like that. I have been busy. You know I wouldn't do that to you."

"I don't want to hear that weak ass shit." India said turning around to walk back up the stairs. She went straight to the bathroom to turn on the shower water.

Kevin was right behind her. "Ma, I know you ain't mad. You know I love you and would never hurt you."

India didn't pay him any attention. Kevin knew he had been slacking on pleasing his woman, but he was busy trying to make sure that his business was strong and good. He knew he had to do something to make up for all the days he been leaving early and coming home late. He leaned into the back of India and started kissing her neck. "Since I have been a bad hubby take your anger out on me." Kevin said smiling into her neck while he softly kissed up to her ear.

India wanted Kevin so bad, but she didn't want him to know it so she pretended she didn't hear him and continued to test her shower water. Kevin being the aggressor he is pulled India towards him and started to suck on her neck harder.

"Why are you always trying to play hard to get?" Kevin whispered in her ear while his hands roamed her hips and breasts.

"Look, ain't no one playing hard to get. I'm trying to take a shower so I can go to bed. " India moaned, loving the feeling of Kevin's lips on her. She moved her head to the side so that he could have more access to her. All of a sudden Kevin took India by her shoulder and pulled her towards the sink, pushing her upper body down in the process. He raised her dress to her waist and dropped his pants. He knew India was wet for him so he entered her hard, just like she liked it. He was giving her long and deep strokes.

"So, who do you love?" Kevin asked while digging deep into India, hitting her spot.

"I love you." India said looking back at Kevin while he went deeper.

While getting in his zone, he slapped her on the ass, and then turned her around so she would face him. While Kevin had India's leg in his arm, his dick ready to go back into her pussy, his cell phone began to ring. India knew he was going to answer the phone so she grabbed his dick and pulled him into her.

"Don't you dare answer that?" India said losing her focus a little. He didn't pay her any mind and picked the phone up.

"Yeah?" Kevin said once he picked up the phone. Never once did he lose his stroke with India. "What? How the fuck did that happen?" The caller was making Kevin angry. He started hitting India with deeper and deeper strokes, grabbing her hip in a vice like grip.

The strokes were catching India off of guard so she said "Babe, what are you doing?"

Kevin looked at her and told the caller "Yo, got to hit you back." Once he got off the phone he kissed India all over her face and continued pleasing her. Kevin reached in between them and starting playing with her clit, rubbing it in fast circles. After a few more minutes of giving it to India, they both exploded together.

India got right in the shower while Kevin picked up his phone and called the caller back. She was happy that she finally got what she wanted. In the middle of enjoying her hot shower, Kevin pulled the curtain back and was just looking at her for a minute then he said "I have to make a run. I'll try and be back soon."

India was mad because she wanted to lay under her man for a change, but she knew he had to make his money. "Are you going to take a shower before you leave?"

"I took one in the other bathroom. Alright ma give me a kiss, I'll be back soon." Kevin leaned towards India and gave her a quick kiss.

"Love you Baby. Be safe." India said once he closed the curtain.

"Love you too ma." Kevin said.

Shortly after she got out of the shower she wanted to know what Kim was doing so she picked up the house phone and called her cell phone. There was no answer.

Chapter 12

Kim

Kim woke up at 5 a.m. to her cell phone ringing. "Oh shit. What time is it? Where am I?" She jumped up quickly, taking in her surroundings as she looked around. She looked at her phone and noticed that it was Quan that called her. She knew she had to call him back quick and explain why she wasn't home. While pressing 2 for speed dial, she looked around and knew where she was at. Everything still looked the same since she moved out.

The phone didn't even ring twice before Quan had answered, "Yo, ma where you at? You got me worried."

"I'm sorry baby, I was sleep. I'm about to come home right now." Kim said, not sure if she had sex with Shawn or not, but she felt so guilty.

"Ok, come on home. I was nervous when you ain't answer my calls and texts. "Quan said relieved.

"I understand. I told you I was going to sleep my liquor off." Kim explained.

"I know ma. I'm going to be up waiting for you." Quan said.

"Ok. I'll be there in a few." Kim said before hanging up.

After getting off the phone with Quan, Kim fell back on the bed and closed her eyes. She tried to recap what happened last night, and then she looked over to her left and saw Shawn sound asleep.

"Kim what did you do?" She asked herself. She knew she had to get out of there and fast. Getting up from the bed she found her jeans which were on the chair that she use to sit in and read while Shawn watched ESPN. Kim was having flashbacks being in Shawn's house. While she was in deep thought, she heard the sheets moving behind her.

"What you doing up baby girl?" Shawn asked sleepily.

"What happened last night?" Kim asked.

"Nothing at all. We were talking and then you fell asleep and I took your clothes off." Shawn said being truthful.

"I have to go." Kim said putting her jeans and shirt on.

"Just stay with me a little while longer. I miss holding you in my arms." Shawn said while pulling Kim back on the bed with him.

Shawn knew what Kim liked and he wasn't going to let her go till she let him please her. He started to kiss Kim on her spot and touched her in places where he knew she liked. Kim was getting into it so much that she had to do something before she ended up having sex with Shawn.

"Shawn stop. I have to go." Kim said breaking away from his grip.

She jumped up so quick and grabbed her shoes and keys and was out the door before he could protest. When she got in the car, she fixed herself up and dialed India's number.

"Hello." Kevin said in a sleepy voice.

"Hey Kev, can I speak to India." Kim asked, gripping her steering wheel.

Kevin woke India up and passed her the phone without saying anything.

India answered angrily cause her rest was broken. "What?"

"Damn, my bad for waking you up." Kim said.

"Bitch it's five in the morning! Why are you calling me this early? Is everything okay?" India asked.

"Indi, I think I made a mistake." Kim said so confused with all the feelings going through her head.

"What you talking about Kim?"

"I'm just leaving Shawn's place." Kim said feeling so bad.

"What… I hope you did not have sex with him Kimberly." India said sounding like her mother.

"No, I didn't but it was close. I feel so bad. I feel like I cheated on Quan and not sure if I should tell him."

"You didn't do anything wrong so just sleep on it and things would get better." India said.

After Kim ended her conversation with India, she was pulled in her drive way. She was nervous and feeling guilty.

She got out of the car and walked in the house. When she made it to the bedroom she saw Quan spread across the bed.

She leaned over and kissed Quan's lips to wake him up.

"Hey baby girl." Quan said when he felt Kim's lips on him.

"Hey love. I thought you were going to stay up and wait for me." Kim said as she took off her clothes and put on her night clothes.

"I was up. You know I can't sleep without you being next to me." Quan said pulling Kim close to him.

"Yeah I know. My baby can't sleep without me next to him." Kim said getting comfortable under Quan.

"So how was the club?" Quan asked.

"It was fun. I'm glad I went out." Kim said falling asleep in Quan arms.

"So, what do you want to do when you wake up baby?" Quan asked Kim but to only get no answer. Kim had fallen asleep.

Chapter 13

Lisa

"I can't believe it's been a week since Shermika called saying she has a baby by my man." While Lisa sat on the bed playing the entire call back in her head, she heard Terence cut the shower water off. When she saw him step out the shower, she thought to herself, *"Should I ask him about the child or should I just fall back and act like I don't know anything?"* While in deep thought, Terence noticed something wasn't right.

"Ay yo baby, what's wrong?" Terence asked showing concern. He noticed that she been acting strange for a week now.

"What?" Lisa asked giving him a face of disgust.

"I asked you are you okay? What was that face for?" Terence asked noticing the face that Lisa made to him.

"Yeah, I'm good." Lisa said getting up to go wake TJ up. Today they were having a family outing. They planned on taking TJ to the zoo because it was a really nice day outside. After everyone got dressed and were ready to leave, they got in the car. TJ was so happy all the way to the zoo. All he kept doing was talking about all the animals he would see. Lisa on the other hand was trying to avoid talking or looking at Terence, so she occupied her time talking to TJ or texting her girls. Terence noticed her behavior but didn't address it. When they pulled up in the zoo parking lot, TJ almost jumped out of his car seat.

Lisa took her attention away from her phone and turned to TJ, "Boy you better sit your butt down before you get a whooping."

TJ calmed down and just looked out the window. Terence found a parking spot and all of them got out. They started walking; Lisa forgot all about Shermika and enjoyed her family day. They went to all the animal houses and TJ got excited every time they went into a new one. They were having fun eating ice cream, looking at animals and just being around each other. After walking to all of the animal houses, they decided to get something to eat. When they entered the eatery, Lisa and TJ found a set while Terence went to get the food. While Terence went and got the food Lisa kept a close eye on him.

After the food was ready, Terence brought the tray of food to the table. They were enjoying their burgers till they heard a female call Terence name. Lisa and Terence looked in the direction of the voice.

"I knew that was you." The girl said walking to the table. She was very beautiful, 5'5" tall, slim, and brown skin with beautiful slanted brown eyes made up her appearance.

"What's up? What you want?" Terence asked not looking at the girl or nothing.

"So that's how we are now?" The girl asked Terence with her hands on her hips.

Lisa was feeling very disrespected and was about to show her ass, but she remembered that her son was sitting across from her.

"Look, I'm with my family. You need to leave." Terence said trying to keep his cool, and not trying to piss Lisa off on something that wasn't serious.

"FAMILY? Let me introduce myself." The girl said. She put her hand out toward Lisa and said. "I'm Shermika, his baby mama. I think we already talked."

Lisa had the look of murder on her face. She wanted to beat Shermika and Terence ass right then and there.

"Yo, you need to chill with telling people that's my baby. What you mean you talked to my wife?" Terence asked looking at Lisa but talking to Shermika.

"So now you are denying our daughter. I knew you weren't shit. I don't want to be with you, all I want you to do is be a father to your child." Shermika said. Deep down she wanted to have the family bond that she just witnessed Terence having with Lisa.

"Yo… Bitc…!" Terence caught his self before he lost his temper.

"Look Shermika. How about we meet up and talk about it later." Lisa said not in the mood for the drama and not in front of her son.

"Yeah, we can do that." Shermika said walking off.

Shermika walked off, Lisa face was red with anger. Terence was mad too because ever since she got pregnant she been putting the blame on him. He knew it wasn't his baby but when she had her baby it had the same complexion as him and some of his features.

"I'm ready to go." Lisa said not in the mood to eat anymore.

"Mommy, I'm not finished." TJ said not understanding what was going on.

Terence knew that Lisa was pissed and all he could do is keep her happy by following her demands.

"Little man your mom ready to go. You can finish in the car." Terence said while picking up TJ's stuff.

The walk to the parking lot was quiet. Lisa face was red and you could see the steam coming from her head.

As soon as they got in the car, Lisa couldn't hold it in any more.

"What the fuck was that about Terence?" Lisa said. She never cursed around TJ but today she was pissed and forgot he was in the back eating his chicken tenders.

"Yo, ma calm down. It ain't nothing." Terence said.

"So, you having a baby by somebody else is nothing. What kind of shit is that?"

"It's not my baby."

"Yeah, that's what they all say. Did you fuck her?" Lisa asked.

Terence was getting pissed off at Lisa now, so he continued to drive.

"I know you heard me. Did you fuck her?"

"Yes, yes, I fucked the bitch. I fucked her before we were talking."

"So how the fuck do I know it's not your baby."

"Because I'm telling you it's not. I fucked her using a condom."

"I don't want to hear that shit. We are going to get a DNA test. If it's yours we are over."

"What? I told you it's not mine. Fuck it if you want a DNA test then you can get one. But, that other shit you talking ain't gonna happen." Terence said driving home and meaning every word that he said.

When they pulled up in the drive way, Lisa walked to her car and drove off leaving TJ and Terence by themselves. She needed to clear her head.

Chapter 14

London

London was enjoying her nice spring weekend, cleaning her house. Every time she cleaned up Bryant would come behind her and mess up, along with BJ. They were pissing London off.

"Look, if you and your son mess up something else again, I'm going to fuck you up." London told BJ.

"Chill shawty, we going to clean up." BJ said to London as he put a cup in the sink.

"Yeah I can't tell! You just added another cup to the sink." London said.

"Look damn it, I'm washing the cup out." BJ said picking up the cup and washing it.

"I don't know who you talking to. You ain't talking to me. I got this. Just leave you are dismissed." London said waving BJ away.

"I know you did not just play me." BJ said.

"Yeah, I did. Now you take your son and y'all find something to do. It's a nice day out."

BJ took Bryant and they left the house to go have some father/son bonding time.

When they left, London felt so relieved. Lately she had been stressed for a number of reasons. Last week Keith called her, she's pressed by BJ to have another baby, and her job pissing her off. To take her mind of her stress, she continued to clean. After the house was spotless, she grabbed a wine cooler and plopped down on the couch and watched TV. As soon as she got comfortable, the phone rang. She was so into the movie she picked up the phone quick.

"Hello?" London said.

"London? What you doing?" Lisa asked.

"Nothing having some alone time." London said.

"I hear that." Lisa said.

"What you doing? Hold on, what's the matter?" London asked noticing something strange in Lisa's voice.

"I'm just driving around trying to clear my head. Today we were doing our family outing and ran into Terence other baby mama that I just found out about a week ago." Lisa informed her.

"What! Terence got another child? How old is the child? Did he tell you?"

"Well, she is four and no, he didn't tell me I found out because she called the house last week but I didn't pay it any mind. Then today she approached us at the zoo with my son. I lost it. I just left the house as soon as we made it home." Lisa had to talk to someone and the first person she thought of was London.

"Dag sis, what did he say?"

"He said it's not his child. So I told him he has to take a DNA test and if it is his I'm out."

"I hear that sis. That's around the time y'all were dating. Do you need me?" London asked.

"Naw, go ahead and enjoy your free time. I'll call you later." Lisa said before hanging up.

London hung up the phone and was about to continue to watch her movie until her stomach started talking to her. She got up and made her something to eat.

When she was done cooking herself something to eat, she went back to the living room and continued her movie which was on demand.

She was so relaxed now she said to herself, "I can get a piece of mind like this." As soon as that left her mouth the phone rang again.

"Who the hell is it now?" London said out loud before she picked up the phone.

"Hello?" London said. There was no answer.

"Hello?" London repeated herself. She could hear breathing, so she hung up the phone.

As soon as she hung up, she looked at the caller id and it was an unknown number.

The phone began to ring again. The same thing happened again. London could hear breathing and got no answers. She was a little spooked by the action that she checked all the windows and doors and cut the ringer off on the phone. After she made sure everything was secure, she was able to relax again.

London was in her zone and watched two movies when she heard the front door open, it caught her off of guard.

"Yo, why you ain't been answering the phone?" BJ asked when he came in the house.

"Hey mommy did you have fun by yourself?" Bryant asked. He had blue sticky stuff all around his mouth.

"Yes honey I had fun. Did you have fun with your daddy?" London asked Bryant not paying attention to BJ.

"Yeah, mommy we went to the playground, ate pop sickles and saw grandma." Bryant told his mom.

"That's great little man." London said smiling at him.

"Yo, little Nigga go upstairs while I talk to your mom for a few." BJ said. He watched his son run up the stairs then turned his gaze to London. "So, why you ain't answer the phone? I have been calling here like crazy." BJ asked.

"I have been getting prank calls all day so I just cut the ringer off." London told BJ.

"What?" He said looking at the phone caller id. He noticed a lot of unknown calls and he started to get pissed because he didn't like anyone playing around with his family.

"What were they saying?" BJ asked gripping the phone tightly.

"They wouldn't say anything. All I could hear was them breathing."

As soon as London said that, the phone rang and the caller id said unknown. BJ answered the phone this time.

"Hello."

"London?" The caller said.

"Yo, who the fuck is this?" BJ asked hearing a man's voice say his woman's name.

"I want London." The caller said.

"Look, Nigga you ain't speaking to London. If you call here again I'm going to find out who you are and fuck you up." BJ said.

"Fuck you Nigga and your bitch." The caller said then hung up.

London looked at BJ nervous because she didn't know who would be calling for her.

"Who was that?" London asked, her legs beginning to shake.

"I don't know baby, but when I find out he's a dead man." BJ said pulling London close to him.

London was happy to have BJ there to protect her. She knew that's why she loved him so much.

Chapter 15

Lorren

Lorren woke up early on Sunday because she told her mom that she, Rico, Lacey and little Rico would go to church with her. As always Rico stayed out late and he was tired, but he knew this is something Lorren wanted to do so he forced his self out the bed.

"Yo, ma how long is this church service?" Rico asked as he put on some slacks that Lorren brought him.

"I don't know. Why what else you have to do?" Lorren asked while getting Lacey dressed.

"I'm just asking damn, calm down." Rico said.

Lorren made sure everyone was dressed and ready; they left and headed to church. The church was packed but they were able to get a seat by Landon, her mother, London and BJ. The service was good. Rico who was never a church person was dozing off a little but Lorren would make sure he didn't fall asleep. When the service was over BJ and Rico were talking in the back of the church while Lorren and London talked to some of the members of the church.

"Man, I saw you dozing off over there." BJ said laughing.

"Man, I'm tired. I didn't want to make mammi mad so I came." Rico said, looking at the church girls that were eyeing him and BJ.

While they were talking, two church girls that were looking at the men the whole service walked over to them.

"Hey, how you doing, I'm Brittany, and this is Monique."

"Hey, I'm Rico and this is BJ."

"So, I see y'all are visitors. Was those y'all girlfriends or y'all friends?" Brittany asked Rico.

Before Rico could respond Lorren was walking up and answered for him. "I'm his wife."

The girl had the stuck face and to make it worst, London called BJ name and he went to her side with the quickness.

"Let's go boy." Lorren said to Rico.

Rico took a deep breath and went with Lorren. He was getting tired of some of the shit Lorren did. They were having dinner at Lorren mother house. When they arrived at Lorren mothers' house they were hungry. While they were waiting for the food to finish cooking, the men were in the living room while the women were in the kitchen. When the food was done, everyone went to the table and they blessed the food. They were enjoying the food till Rico phone rang.

"Hello?" Rico answered without hesitation. "I'm with my fam….Oh for real? Give me a half hour and I will be there. Alright see you in a few. Peace." Rico hung up his phone and continued to eat.

Lorren wasn't going to say anything but she wanted to know who he was talking to and where he was going. "So, who was that?"

"One of my people." Rico said trying to avoid an argument.

"So, where you going in a half hour?" Lorren asked.

"I have a few runs to make. That's it." Rico said taking a deep breath.

Lacey didn't want them to start at the table so she said "How about you two dismiss yourself from the table and handle your problems."

Rico and Lorren got up from the table and walked to Lorren and London old room.

"Ma, why you starting stuff?" Rico asked closing the door.

"You always leaving me lately and I think it's somebody else." Lorren said.

"Why would you think that?"

"Like I said I barely see you, that girl calling your phone. So, I'm not good enough for you anymore?" Lorren asked sitting on the bed.

"Look, the girl that called my phone is my best friend Maria. We grew up together and she just moved back to DC two weeks ago. She moved to Florida when I started talking to you. I love you baby. I would never cheat on you. I'm too jealous to cheat on you because I won't want you to do it to me."

"Why you ain't just tell me who she was?" Lorren asked.

"Because, just as jealous as I am you are worse." Rico said sitting next to Lorren on the bed. He started placing kisses on Lorren's neck and rubbing in between her thighs. Lorren loved Rico lips and so did her body. She didn't care if she was in her mother's house. It wasn't the first time she had sex there. That was how she got pregnant with little Rico.

Rico was glad that Lorren wore a dress to church. Pushing Lorren to her back on the bed, Rick moved over her. He placed his hand under her dress and pulled her panties off. Using one hand to unbuckle his pants and push his boxers down, he used the other to check Lorren's readiness for him. In one quick thrust, Rico was inside her to the hilt. He and Lorren were so caught up into each other that they almost forgot that they were in her mothers' house. While Rico was giving Lorren long deep thrusts, he made it his business to make sure that she knew who the boss of the relationship was.

"Are you going to start trusting me?" Rico asked as he gave Lorren a deep hard stroke.

"Yes." Lorren said in pleasure.

"Who you love?" once again Rico hit her with the same move.

"I love you." Lorren said with her legs shaking from the pleasure.

"That's what a Nigga need to hear." Rico said never losing his stroking pattern. He was giving her long and deep strokes. Hitting her G-spot, making her fill up in ecstasy.

After he hit her spot a couple of times, they both came together. Yet again Rico busted inside of Lorren.

Trying to catch their breath, Rico grabbed Lorren face and said "I need you to trust me. I don't need all of this mouth that you give me cause it only just make me want to go back to my old self."

"I do trust you, but I don't know how I would react if you cheat on me." Lorren said.

"Well, if you ever cheat on me I would kill you." Rico said with a straight face.

"Yeah, well I feel the same way so don't let it happen, ok?" Lorren said giving Rico a kiss on the lips and getting up so she can go wash up in the bathroom.

After they got cleaned up, they went back down stairs to only stay for a few minutes. After saying their goodbyes they headed home. When they got in the house, Rico remembered he had somewhere to be.

"Alright, mami I'm out. See you later." He said to Lorren, then gave her and the kids a kiss.

"Where are you going?" Lorren asked.

"I'm going out with my other girlfriend." Rico said to Lorren then walked out the door.

All Lorren could do was storm up the stairs and get her kids ready for school tomorrow.

Chapter 16

Danni

It was a bright Monday morning when Danni woke up. She had to take Genesis to day care and be at the hospital since she had a lot of patients for the day.

Moe woke up when he heard Danni moving around the room. "Where are you going this early in the morning?" He asked looking at Danni.

"I'm going to work and taking lil man to day care." Danni replied.

"Oh well, if you wait a few I could drive you to work and stuff." Moe said getting up.

"Naw, go ahead and get your rest. You can pick Gen up from day care today." Danni said pulling her hair back in a ponytail.

"Cool with me baby. I'll take you to lunch okay." Moe said laying back down.

Danni went and gave Moe a peck then went and picked Genesis up and headed out the door.

After dropping Genesis off, Danni rushed and got some breakfast and headed right to the hospital. When she walked in, she always caught the eyes of men looking at her. She saw her friend Jaden who was so crazy. He thought all the men were after him even when they were straight.

"Hello Miss Danielle Moore." Jaden said loud when Danni walked through the doors.

"Hello to you to Mr. Jaden Brown." Danni said smiling.

"Oh excuse me you know I am MISS Jaden Brown." Jaden said flinging his hair over his shoulder.

"Yeah, I know diva. So, how many coochies are you looking at today Miss.?" Danni asked biting into her breakfast sandwich.

"I see Miss Danni have jokes today. Any who, I have 6 coochies to look at today. Who would ever think that this diva was going to make a living looking between a woman legs. I am so under paid." Jaden said.

Danni was laughing so hard at Jaden that she almost forgot she was in the work place. While Jaden and Danni were laughing so hard and cracking jokes, their advisor walked through the door.

"What's so funny?" the advisor said.

Both Danni and Jaden stop laughing and said "nothing" at the same time.

"Gurl, let's get started before our ass be fired." Jaden said.

Danni saw two patients before her advisor came and told her she had a visitor. Danni went to the lounge and saw two police officers. Her heart started to beat fast and she became nervous.

"Danielle Moore?" the young officer asked.

"Yes?" Danni answered nervously.

"My partner and I want to ask you some questions about Bryon Miller."

"Okay." Danni said showing no signs of being nervous suddenly as she sat down.

"What was your relation to Mr. Miller?"

"I was his girlfriend."

"How long did you all date?"

"We dated for about 4 years."

"Why did you both separate?"

"He was abusive and I was hospitalized. I left him after that."

"So, Miss Moore why are there no records of you being abused."

"I never pressed charges. But when I went to the hospital I had to report what was wrong with me."

"So are you currently dating?"

"Yeah, I am."

"Who are you dating?"

"Excuse me, but I thought you wanted to ask questions about Bryon. Not my dating habits."

The older cop who looked nasty, stood up and got in Danni's face. "Look you little bitch. I know you had something to do with Mr. Miller's death."

Danni was shocked to hear a cop talk to her like that. "I have nothing to do with it. The only thing I have to do with it is staying with someone who whopped my ass for fun."

"All fingers point to you. You had a reason to kill him, and when I prove that you did it, I'm going to put you under the jail. Oh and by the way, your son Genesis would be in foster care, and your boyfriend Maurice Powell will be right next to you, rotting in jail." The older cop said.

"I think this questioning is over." Danni stood up and excused herself.

Danni was so fucked up in the head the rest of the morning. She needed to clear her mind and before she knew it, it was time for her to go to lunch with Moe.

He was waiting for Danni outside of the hospital when it was time for her lunch break. When she got in the car, Moe noticed that something was wrong with her.

"What's wrong babe?" Moe asked driving towards T.G.I. Friday's.

"Well, two officers came to my job and questioned me about Bryon." She replied, looking straight ahead.

"What kind of questions they asked you?" Moe asked getting mad.

"They asked my relation with Bryon, then told me I had something to do with his death and told me that you and I are going to be in prison next to each other. They even said they were going to put my baby in foster care." Danni said, starting to cry.

"D, don't worry about what they say. They just talking. Ain't nothing going to happen to me, you or our son. I promise. Do you trust me?" Moe asked taking his eyes off the road to wipe at Danni's face with his finger.

"Yes, I trust you." Danni said feeling better because she knew that Moe won't allow anything or anybody to hurt them.

"Ok, well, stop tripping and let's have the best time on this lunch date. Maybe we can skip lunch and you can give me some afternoon pussy." Moe said on the sly.

Danni smiled at Moe before replying, "Well, I guess just this once. But I'm still going to be hungry."

"I already got it covered." Moe drove to a hotel.

When they arrived at the hotel, Moe led Danni to the room. When she opened the door she saw food was already on a table centered in the room.

Smirking at Moe over her shoulder, she asked, "So, you already had this planned?"

"Yeah, something slight." Moe said laughing.

They ate the lunch with conversation in between. When they were done Moe placed his napkin down and looked at Danni. "Now can I eat you?"

Danni smiled seductively. Moe took Danni's clothes off and placed her on the bed. Spreading her legs, he kissed her inner thighs on both sides before diving in and sucking her clit into his mouth. Moe ate Danni out as if she would be his last meal ever. Pushing her legs farther apart, Danni looked down to see Moe's head moving back and forth, rotating between her clit and pussy lips. The motion alone caused Danni's legs to start shaking. Not even a minute later she was cumming, grabbing Moe's head to ride out her orgasm. Moe leaned back and switched positions so that Danni was now on top of him. It was easy for her to sink onto his dick since she was still wet. She began to ride him, moaning loudly when he kept rubbing against her spot. They were so into their love making that Danni forgot she was on her lunch break. Her cell phone rung and knocked them out of her zone.

Reaching for it on the floor, she answered out of breath, "Hello."

"Miss. Moore, I know you better bring your ass back. You have five minutes before your break is over." Jaden said.

"Oh, shit. Here I come. Cover for me please." Danni said moaning softly when Moe started to press on her clit.

"Ok honey. Oh by the way bust your nut girl and tell sexy Moe I said Hey."

Danni laughed at Jaden then got off the phone. "Babe, we have to go." Danni jumped up off of Moe.

"Yo, ma I ain't even come yet." Moe said, looking down at his glistening, stiff dick.

Danni was in the bathroom washing up. "I know but we'll continue when I get home."

Moe sucked his teeth as he gathered his clothes, "Man, iight. Let's go."

Moe dropped Danni off back at the hospital and she promised to finish when she got home.

Chapter 17

Tracey

Tracey sat back in her classroom waiting for the bell to ring so she can get far away from the school. It was two fights and she had to deal with some ghetto ass parents today and she wasn't feeling that at all. She was on the verge of fighting her damn self. All she was thinking about was getting out of the school and hitting a jay.

As soon as the bell rung the kids ran out the class and Tracey was right behind them. She sat in her car and thought about who she would ask to smoke with her. She thought about all her friends and knew they all were busy at the time. Then she remembered that Staci took off today, so she called her.

"Hello" Staci answered.

"Hey girl! What you up to?" Tracey asked starting up her car.

"Shit, just watching TV. What you up to?" Staci asked.

"About to light up cause I had a long day at work." Tracey said stopping at a store on the corner.

"True, I hear that." Staci said.

"You trynna get down." Tracey asked, and then said to the cashier "Can I get two grape cigarillos?"

"Hell yeah, I'm trying to get down. What you need?" Staci asked.

"Girl, I got everything. I'll be there in a few." Tracey said leaving out the store and heading to her car to go to Staci house.

When she got to Staci house, she made sure that Zoe would pick Handsome up from day care and told him she would be chilling with Staci. Tracey knocked on the door and Staci answered.

"What up bitch." Staci said when she opened the door for Tracey.

"Ain't shit hoe, so you roll up one and I'll do the other." Tracey said as she sat down on the couch.

"That's cool."

"Oh yeah don't be making no fuck boys like your damn sister." Tracey said, remembering the time all of her girls were smoking and Danni wanted to roll and fucked the blunt up.

"Girl, you know I never roll fuck boys and for my sister you should have known not to let her ass roll." They both started to laugh.

After a few minutes both of the blunts were rolled and they started a rotation up. Tracey had the *"purp"* which she got from her brother Tone. They were high as hell, when they finish smoking.

"Nigga, that shit was good." Staci said to Tracey.

Tracey looked over at Staci, her eyes barely opened, "Hell yeah, I'm high as fuck."

"Where you get that from?"

"From my brother." When Tracey said that, her phone rung and it was India.

"Hello." Tracey said.

"Bitch, what it do?" India asked.

"Shit at Staci house, high as a mug."

"Shit, y'all ain't invite me. That's fucked up."

"Bitch you was at the firm. So don't fake. Why the hell you call me?"

"I called to let you know about Kevin party which is Saturday. Let Staci know too. I was going to call her next but you with her. Oh yeah we plan on having a spa day early Saturday morning to prepare for the party. I already made y'all hair appointments." India said.

"Damn, well y'all got the shit all planned out. Oh Staci said she getting her hair braided Saturday morning, so she would make it to the party and pre party." Tracey said.

"That's what's up. Oh yeah for the pre party bring some of that fire. We are going to get twisted." India said.

"I got you girl." Tracey said then hung up the phone.

Tracey and Staci were watching "You so Crazy" by Martin and cracking up. The standup was so funny. Tracey felt around for her phone when she heard it ring again.

"Hello" She asked without looking at the caller id.

"Hey beautiful, how you been?" Tracey was caught off of guard by the voice.

"Hey Kenny, how you doing?" Tracey said.

"I'm good now that I hear your voice." Kenny said making Tracey blush.

"That's good to hear. I've been well myself." Tracey said trying to hide that she was high.

"That's what's up. So I take it that you are happy with your man now?" Kenny asked. Tracey almost dropped the phone from his question. The last thing she wanted to talk about with Kenny was her relationship.

"Yes, I'm happy with my man. I see you had a child like you wanted." Tracey said.

"Well to be honest that was my godson. I never found another woman worthy of being the mother of my child." Kenny said.

"Oh." That was the only thing that Tracey could say back. She wasn't expecting that answer.

"Can I take you out some day?" Kenny asked.

"I'll let you know if we can work something out."

"Ok, beautiful, don't forget about me." Kenny said with a smile in his voice.

"I won't." Tracey hung up the phone, feeling hot and bothered.

"So, I take it that that was Kenny." Staci said.

"Yes girl, he might was a square but he could fuck like shit. Plus he looked good. I ran into him at the circus."

"Damn, weren't you with Zoe?"

"Yes girl and Zoe wanted to whop his ass. I wasn't going to let him do that though." Tracey said.

Tracey was sitting there and kept thinking about how smooth Kenny's voice was on the phone. She couldn't take the heat that was overwhelming her body.

"Girl, I'm about to go." Tracey said to Staci.

"Where you about go?" Staci asked, looking over at her curiously.

"Girl I'm about to go home. I got to get my dick wet."

"Bitch you dumb. Go ahead and get your dick wet then. Shit, get it in for me too."

Tracey got up and got in her car. All the way home she thought about all the ways that she and Kenny use to get it on. Then she remembered why she left him. Switching her thoughts to Zoe, she was going to give her man the best sex he ever had as soon as she saw him.

Chapter 18

What a Party

Kevin was celebrating his birthday right this year. He had everything planned to the T and was going to rent out the club "Move", which was owned by BJ and Terence. Everybody who is well known around the city was going to be there. People were willing to spend bread to go. If a lady was looking for a baller the, party was the place to be. If a man was looking for a fly chick Kevin's party would be packed with them.

The Ladies...

The girls planned a trip to the mall, nail, and hair salon. They went to the mall first and shopped for two hours to find the best freak'em dress. After they found the right dress, they headed to the nail salon. They got the full treatment, nails, toes and eyebrows. They knew that their hair had to be last because they needed it to be fresh. When they got to the hair salon it wasn't crowded because India had let everybody stylists know that they would come in today and they were press on time.

"Oh my look who it is." Ebony the stylist said when the girls walked into the salon.

"Bitch you fake." India said as she sat down in Ebony's chair.

"Oh no Miss Indi, not using that language in my salon." Ebony said rolling her neck.

Everybody started laughing because Ebony was the one who was the biggest bitch caller in the whole salon. Every girl had their same stylist since they have been coming to "Ebony's hair salon". Kim stylist was the biggest Diva named Jess, but he could do some hair. Lorren went to Ashley who was quiet most of the time. All she does is laugh at the other stylist while they joke around and stuff. London went to Tia who was the one who thought she was the superstar of the salon. Danni went to Brittany who had a boyfriend that called the salon every hour for stupid stuff. Lisa went to Stephanie, who was the church girl since her and Lisa always talking about church. Last, Tracey went to Quetta, who was ghetto as hell. She always had something to talk about because she knew everybody business and didn't have a problem spreading it either.

"Oh my Lord. I don't need to hear this language." Stephanie said.

"Shut up Steph. You be faking like you all holier than thou." Jess said. The whole salon started to laugh.

"Kimmie, what you want done to this mess?" Jess asked, picking up strands of her hair and examining it.

"Colored, straighten, and flat iron. You think you can handle that?" Kim asked, looking at Jess in the mirror with her right eyebrow risen.

Everything was cool in the salon. It was a lot of chatter as always. That changed when Quetta asked Kim about the rumors she had heard on the street.

"Yo Kim." Quetta said.

"What's up?" Kim answered annoyed because she already knew she wanted to know something.

"Is it true that Quan and Shawn are brothers?" Quetta asked curling Tracey hair.

"Naw, it's not true." Kim said knowing that Quetta had a big mouth.

"Oh ok girl. Cause I was about to say that is nasty if they were." Quetta said.

"Bitch, I know you ain't saying shit is nasty. Bitch you established the word nasty." Tracey said having her girl back.

"So, are you still talking to Shawn?" Brittany asked.

Before Kim could say anything London jumped in.

"No, she ain't talking to that no good motherfucker. If she ever talk back to that nigga she is a dumb ass."

Kim forgot that Jess had the flat iron in his hand and turned to face London.

"First off Ms. London, I am tired of your shit. You always have something bad to say about him. You don't know shit. Oh and for calling someone dumb, bitch you need to look in the mirror. You have a fucking good ass man who loves your stuck up ass and you treating him like shit. Bitch you sitting here worrying about other people's relationship when you need to focus on your own, DUMB ASS." Kim said and turned back in the chair so Jess could finish her hair. London just sat back quiet because she knew she was wrong.

"Any who, what's up with this party tonight?" Lorren asked trying to clear the tension. She knew her sister had a habit of doing that shit because she always does it to her.

"Girl, I'm going to be up in that party with my freak'em dress on." Jess said, dancing with his tongue out. Everyone in the salon started to laugh.

"Boy, you dumb." Danni said still laughing.

They were finally finished around 7PM. Everyone decided to meet at Tracey's house so they could get ready and pre-game. They knew they weren't going to arrive to the party till 12AM. After leaving the salon, India dropped Kim off at her house. As soon as Kim got in the house she went upstairs to wash her face because it felt sticky from the salon. Then she heard her name being called.

"Yeah." She yelled towards the stairs.

"Damn, you don't let anybody know you home." Quan asked walking up the stairs to her.

"I had to wash my face. Why were you yelling?" Kim asked putting her outfit out.

Quan eyed Kim and the dress she had in her hand, "Cause I didn't know if that was you. Where you going with that short ass dress?"

"To the party for Kev. It's not even that short." Kim said not paying him any attention.

"Whatever. Oh I have some rules for your ass while you at this party."

Kim looked over at Quan and started laughing, "Rules? You ain't my daddy nigga."

"Yeah rules. I don't have to be your daddy, I'm your man." Quan said.

"You my man, what that mean?" Kim asked because she don't like to be on restrictions.

"Look I don't have time for this. I have to meet up with my mans. These are the rules: first, Shawn going to be there so stay away from him. Second, don't be flirting. Third, don't get fucked up. Lastly, don't show your ass. You understand?" Quan said.

Walking towards the bathroom, Kim waved off his demands, "Whatever Quan."

"Kim, don't walk away from me, I told you about that."

"And I told you about acting like you are my father."

"Yo, I don't feel like fussing, just do those things. I love you."

"Yeah whatever."

"I'll see you at the party, iight ma." Quan said to Kim as he walked up behind her. Kim just looked at him. Quan gave her a kiss and was out the door.

All the girls did the necessary so they could be on point for the party. They ended up meeting at Tracey's house at 10. India and Kim brought the liquor, while Tracey had the weed. They were ready to get the party started. All the girls wore sweats and a t-shirt so their clothes wouldn't smell like the weed.

"Kim." London said to Kim when they were making their drinks.

"What's up?" Kim asked not looking up from her cup.

London took a deep breath and looked Kim in the eye, "I want to apologize. I didn't mean to say that earlier at the salon.

I know I can be a bitch sometimes, but I just wanna make sure that you are good more than anything. You know you my sis."

"I know and I'm sorry for putting you on the spot like that. I'm not sorry for what I said though, but I know you just wanna look out for me. I love you regardless lil' boy" Kim said.

"Love you too, big boy." London said smiling.

In the living room, Tracey and Staci had rolled three blunts and put them in rotation. Everyone had a cup in hand and were dancing to the music that was playing. Some of the girls were looking at Kim since they noticed she was drinking more than usual. While everyone else had maybe 2 cups, Kim was working on her 4th.

"Yo, Kim. Why you drinking like that?" Lisa asked exhaling the smoke from the jay.

"Because I'm stressed out." Kim said drinking out of her cup.

"What's up?" Tracey asked walking over to her.

Kim rolled her eyes and sipped some more from her cup, "Girl, Quan is tripping hard. This nigga gave me fucking rules for the party. Like I'm his teenage daughter or some shit."

Everyone started laughing. If it was one thing the girls could agree on, rules from men were not taken seriously.

"Rules? What kind of rules?" India asked still laughing.

Using her hand, Kim named off Quan's rules to her friends, "Stay away from Shawn, no flirting, don't get drunk, and don't show my ass."

Staci gave Kim the screwed up face when she asked, "What is wrong with that man?"

"Girl, I have no idea." Kim said shaking her head. "That's how I was when and before he met me so I told him yeah whatever. I'm grown. I don't follow no rules but my own."

"I hear that. Have your fun." London said.

The girls decided to drink some more before they washed up and got dressed. They were looking fly with their short freak'em dresses on and their pumps. Every one of them had on something that showed off their skin. It was either breast or ass showing. Once their make-up was finished they left out of Tracey's house. Everyone piled into Lisa and London's cars since they decided to drive for the night.

Pulling up to the club at 11:30 the line was long as hell. The girls pulled in the front of the club and had valet park the cars. After getting their VIP bands, they walked in the club. Immediately they could sense the envy from some of the girls and the lust from the men.

"Damn this shit is packed." Lorren said looking around.

"Fuck yeah." Tracey said.

They walked to VIP and saw their men. The ladies eyes were low as hell, but Kim was the most fucked up. She was laughing at random stuff.

"What I tell you?" Quan asked Kim when they sat down by them.

"I do not remember what you said to me earlier sir." Kim said speaking properly to Quan.

All of her friends started laughing hard as hell because they knew Kim was going to piss him off just because.

"What is wrong with you?" Quan asked knowing that Kim was trying to be funny.

"Look, I'm trying to have fun tonight, trying to celebrate my motherfucking brother's birthday. So, how about we act like we single tonight." Kim said.

That caught Quan off of guard. "That's what you want. Fine." Quan got up and left from VIP.

Kim shrugged her shoulders and looked at her friends, "Ladies lets party."

They went to the bar and did a couple of rounds of shots. They were ready to cut up and act like they didn't have boyfriends in the club. Hitting the dance floor, the girls started dancing with dudes left and right.

As things were going smooth it always has to be something that causes a good party to go bad.

Tracey was bunned up with Zoe at a table. They were in their own world when she noticed Zoe nose started to flare.

Looking at him quizzically she asked, "What's wrong with you baby?"

"Why is that punk motherfucker here?" Zoe asked keeping an eagle eye on his target.

"Who?" Tracey asked trying to follow his eyes.

"That bitch ass nigga you used to talk to." Zoe said with his still straight ahead.

93

Tracey heart fell. She knew Zoe wanted to fuck Kenny up. "I don't know. But you know this party was talked about everywhere."

"Well, let that nigga say one word to you and see what happen." Zoe said squeezing Tracey's hip.

Tracey was scared. Not for herself but for Kenny because Zoe had his crew with him too. She just continued to entertain Zoe so he could take his focus off Kenny.

Lisa on the other hand was sitting at the bar with Lorren. Their feet had started to hurt. Even though they were going through shit with their man they didn't let that stop them from having fun. They kept a close eye on their boyfriends. Lisa saw Shermika walk towards Terence while he was talking to the DJ.

"Yo, if she touches my man, I'm going to fuck her up and then beat his ass for letting her touch him." Lisa said to Lorren with her fists clenched.

"Who?" Lorren said not paying attention to Terence but looking at Rico.

"That bitch." Lisa pointed. Lorren looked at the girl that Lisa had a death glare on.

"Oh, I feel you girl. I'm just waiting for one girl to go up to Rico. It's going to be on." Lorren said.

Terence saw Shermika standing by the DJ booth but didn't give her time to say anything, "Yo don't want to hear it. Leave me alone." He said and walked away.

In the VIP section London took note of what Kim said to her at the salon and realized that she was being selfish towards

94

BJ. London stayed up under BJ in their own world. They were having fun by their selves in the VIP section. Danni and Moe who couldn't even keep their hands off of each other were having their fun in VIP as well. Danni was getting hot and bothered as Moe talked dirty in her ear and rubbed up and down her body, trying to put us hand up her dress.

"Yo ma let's roll. I had enough of this party shit. I'm trying to have my own private party." Moe said to Danni in her ear.

"Oh Really?" Danni asked smiling.

"Yeah." He said putting his hand up her dress.

"Okay I'm ready. Let me tell my girls I'm gone." Danni got up and walked to find her girls so she could leave. The way Moe was making her feel, she doubted they would make it home.

"Ok meet me back here." Moe said winking at her.

Danni walked down the stairs to the main floor where all her girls were at the bar now except Tracey and London.

"Ok ladies it was nice but I'm about to roll." Danni said hugging them. While Danni was saying her goodbyes, Moe was telling his crew he was about to leave.

Noticing Quan looked tense, he walked up to him and said "Yo Q, what's wrong?"

"Man, her. Look at her." He said to Moe pointing to Kim.

"What? She having fun." Moe said looking at Kim dance.

"Dawg she has on that short ass dress and acting like a damn fool. She just pissing me off. Man she even had the nerve to say we single tonight." Quan was venting to Moe.

"Look man, she just trying to have fun. You know who she loves. She just said that cause you tried to control her. She letting you know she's her own woman." Moe said.

"I feel you. There go lil mama." Quan said when he saw Danni walking up.

"Later Brother." Danni said to Quan.

After Danni left the club, London and BJ disappeared upstairs to his office.

Kim continued to drink and have fun when all of a sudden *"pop champagne remix"* came on. She got on top of the bar and when Lil Kim part came on she start rapping it and dancing as if she was Lil Kim. The dudes were screaming and cheering as if she was a stripper. She was doing nothing but dancing but the dudes loved the show. She caught the attention of Shawn and Quan. Shawn was talking to Kevin and stopped talking when Kim caught his gaze.

"What the fuck is she doing?" Shawn said to Kevin.

"I don't know dawg. I think we need to get her down before your brother fuck her up." Kevin said watching Quan make his way to Kim.

"He ain't going to do shit to her." Shawn said getting up and walking towards the bar.

By time they made it out of VIP, Quan was at the bar. He was pushing his way up to where Kim was at.

"Yo son what you think you doing?" some random guy said to Quan.

Quan was already on fire and pissed off that he just knocked the dude out with one punch. Everyone was shocked. India, Jasmine, Staci, Lorren and Lisa were at the bar with Kim. They were making sure she didn't fall or any dude try and grab her. The girls had never seen Quan so angry to the point that he knocked someone out with one punch.

"Kim." Quan yelled her name with so much bass that she stopped dancing and looked at him. "Get your ass off the bar now."

Kim climbed down from the bar to face Quan. When she got off the bar, he grabbed her arm. Before he could get anywhere, the bouncer was there.

"Yo Q. you can't be knocking niggas out in the club man. What you want me to do with this nigga that's spread out across the floor." The bouncer asked, looking down at the dude on the floor.

Still holding Kim's arm he said "I don't give a fuck. Throw that nigga in the alley."

Quan had Kim by the arm pulling her through the crowd. They ended up in the back where they kept the bottles.

"Get off of me. You are hurting my arm." Kim said, trying to pry Quan's death grip from her arm.

Pulling Kim to stand in front of him against the wall, he looked at her with rage. "What the fuck is your problem."

Looking him directly in the eyes she replied, "I don't have one."

"I should just smack the shit out of you. You acting like a fucking hoe. I have my people in this party. How you think that make me look?"

"Look Quan, I don't care how it makes you look. If I'm embarrassing you so much why don't you just go home?" Kim said.

"I swear to God, you are about to make me fuck you up." Quan said turning red in the face.

Before Kim could say something Shawn walked in.

"Yo bro, I think you need to calm down." Shawn said.

Turning towards Shawn, he yelled, "Man you need to mind your fucking business."

"She is my business. She might be your woman, but she is the mother to my son." Shawn said stepping to Quan.

"Man I don't give a fuck about you. Stay the fuck away from my wife punk ass nigga." Quan said stepping to Shawn too.

"I swear if you weren't my brother you would be in a body bag."

"Nigga fuck you. Act like we ain't brothers and jump."

Shawn didn't want to get into it with Quan. All he just wanted to do is make sure that Kim was good. Kim couldn't watch them anymore as they started to square up with each other.

"Look Quan, I was just trying to have fun. I'm sorry for embarrassing you but trynna control me and threats that you giving me I don't like it. So I'm going to excuse myself from back here and I'm not coming home tonight." Kim said. She didn't give Quan anytime to say anything before she left out leaving both of the men she loved behind.

•

Terence had Lisa close to him as the DJ switched the tune to slow jams. They were minding their business when Shermika ruined their moment again.

"Look who it is. The happy family." Shermika said with envy in her voice.

"I am getting tired of your shit bitch." Lisa said showing the hood side of her. "I tried to be nice to you, but now I see you ain't shit but a hating ass bitch."

"Girl, you better watch what you say before I whip your ass." Shermika said.

"Bitch whip who ass." Lisa said. "I wish you would even think about laying a finger nail on me and see if I don't mop the floor with your ass."

Lisa swung at Shermika so fast that neither she nor Terence saw it coming, connecting with her jaw. Terence grabbed Lisa and pulled her away before she started fighting. He signaled the bouncer to put Shermika out.

•

Lorren on the other hand was still keeping an eye on Rico, when she saw a cute Spanish girl walk up to him and give him a hug. That shit pissed her off. She walked over to where they were. She wanted to know why he was all smiling and shit in the girl's face.

"So who the fuck is this?" Lorren said as soon as she approached Rico who was sitting at a table. The question was directed at Rico but she was staring a hole in the girl's face.

"Mami calm down. This is my best friend Maria. Maria this is Lorren. You finally get to meet her." Rico said making introductions.

Extending her hand to shake Lorren's, she asked, "How you doing? I heard a lot about you."

"I'm sorry. I'm good." Lorren said shaking the hand she offered.

All of a sudden a guy tapped Lorren on the shoulder. She turned around and recognized him immediately. It was her friend Mat who grew up with her and London, but had gotten locked up for 8 years. "Oh my goodness Mat, when did you get out?" Lorren asked as she jumped up and down and gave him a hug.

"Last week. I didn't know you would be at this party." Mat said smiling and looking Lorren up and down.

Rico noticed the look he was giving Lorren and stood up to stand next to her. "Who the fuck is you?" Rico asked Mat looking him up and down.

"This is my friend Mat baby. We grew up together. I haven't seen him in 8 years." Lorren said making introductions. "Mat this is my boyfriend Rico."

"Nice to meet you man. You got a winner right here. Make sure you keep this one close." Mat said.

"Yeah I know." Rico said pulling Lorren closer to him.

"It was nice meeting you Rico, and Lorren it's always a pleasure of seeing you." Mat said smiling at her as he walked off.

Rico was about to show his jealous ways again so he told Lorren they were leaving.

Meanwhile, at the bar were Jasmine, Peaches, Tracey and India were they were grooving to the music. Tracey was waiting for Zoe because she was about to leave when she saw Kenny walking towards them with a dude.

"Oh shit why is Kenny coming over here?" Tracey said to her girls.

"I use to fuck with the dude with him. It's about to be more drama." India said.

"Who you telling." Tracey said rolling her eyes.

Kenny walked up and India turned her head so the dude wouldn't say anything to her. India tried to spark up a conversation with Jasmine and Peaches.

"Where is Kim?" India asked.

"I don't know. Last time she was with Quan, but I saw him leave the club." Jasmine said shrugging.

"Yeah, Kevin told me that he left. So we need to find her cause I know she is fucked up." India said.

"I'll be back." Jasmine said getting off her stool to find her cousin.

When she did that it was an opportunity for India old fuck partner to have a seat.

"So, you don't remember me India?" He asked staring at India.

"Yeah, I remember you." India said.

"I remember your sweet ass. I remember how you use to ride this dick and let me hit it from the back. The moans you used to make... Damn I miss that." He said putting his hand on her thigh.

"Look, move your hand." India said smacking his hand away.

"Oh so it's like that. How about you let me fuck you again? You just cut a nigga off. No call, text or smoke signal."

While India was being harassed, she was hoping that Peaches or Jasmine came back soon. Even though Tracey was right there, Kenny had her attention.

Zoe and Kevin were busy talking about business as they walked towards their women, not taking in the actual scene. While they were talking and walking Jasmine stopped them.

"Y'all saw Kim?" She asked.

Both of them said "no, ask Shawn."

Jasmine left to find Shawn who was in VIP.

"What's up cuz?" Shawn asked Jasmine when he walked up to her.

"I'm looking for Kim. Have you seen her?" Jasmine asked.

"Naw, she walked away from me."

"Well, can you help me find her? I know she didn't leave with Quan because he left by his self."

Shawn got up and looked for Kim. Jasmine went into the bathrooms and walked around to scope the area. Shawn found her sleep on a couch in the back of the second VIP room which wasn't being used.

While Shawn made sure Kim was good. Zoe and Kevin had finished their business talk and headed to the bar where their women were. Zoe noticed that Tracey was pushing Kenny back from her.

"Kenny please just leave. You are drunk and I have a man." Tracey said pushing against his chest.

"Fuck your man." Kenny said.

Right next to them the dude was still trying hard at India.

"Look I'm going to need you to leave me alone." India said, getting more and more annoyed the longer he was in next to her.

"Come on. You know you want to fuck." The guy said.

"Yo, I'm committed. So leave me alone."

The dude laughed and said "once a hoe always a hoe."

"Excuse me?" India said.

The dude stood up in India face as if he was going to try something. Kevin and Zoe approached at the right time. Zoe looked at Kenny and stood toe to toe. Zoe had muscles and looked like he would kill Kenny with one punch.

"Why are you in my girls face?" Zoe asked.

"What it look like nigga. We talking." Kenny said not backing down.

While you could see the steam coming off of Zoe and Kenny, Kevin heard India say excuse me.

"What you say to my girl?" Kevin asked the dude.

"I said once a hoe..." the guy didn't even get the rest out before Kevin hit him.

After Zoe heard the punch that Kevin gave to the guy, he punched the shit out of Kenny. All four of them started fighting in the middle of the party. India and Tracey didn't know what to do but move out the way. The guy that Kevin was fighting was Kenny's cousin and they came with another guy. When the other guys noticed that it was their people fighting they ran over to the fight. Shawn had Kim in his arms sleep when he noticed that Kevin and Zoe were fighting. Shawn put her back down on the couch and ran towards the fight, along with BJ and Terence. The fight escalated quick and more and more people started fighting. The bouncers rushed and broke it up immediately before anything could get damaged. They put the people who were with Kenny out.

"Yo, party over." Kevin said over the microphone beyond pissed.

Everyone was pissed because they were having fun. The party wasn't supposed to be over till 4AM but they ended up shutting it down at 3. The bouncers made sure that everyone left the club. Kevin knew he had to make sure everything was okay before he left.

"Yo babe, who you rode with?" Kevin asked.

"I rode with London." India said.

"Ladies I think y'all should leave." Kevin said.

"I'm not leaving till he ready to go." London said pointing to BJ.

"Look just go ahead. I'll be home soon." BJ said.

The girls weren't hearing that.

"Who did Kim ride with?" Shawn asked.

"She rode with me too." London said.

"Well, she needs to go. She doesn't need to be in here." Shawn said.

"I'll take care of her, but I didn't drive. I rode with my girl and she left. I was going to ride with Lisa." Jasmine said.

Kevin looked at Shawn and said "Yo, go ahead and take care of baby girl, I got this."

"You sure?" Shawn asked. He ain't want to leave his mans like that.

"Yeah son, she's gone." Kevin said laughing a little.

105

Shawn picked Kim up off the couch and he gave each of her friends a kiss on the cheek, and dapped his friends up.

He shook Kim a little and said "You going to tell everybody bye?"

Still drunk and sleep she said "bye" and fell back to sleep.

They all laughed as Shawn, Kim and Jasmine left.

The fellas made sure the club was clean before they headed out. They walked to the cars because the valet brought their keys to them. As soon as they hit the door of the club everyone was booed up. They told the bouncers bye and walked on. Two seconds later gun shots rang out in the air. Every dude protected their girl. Kevin wished he hadn't left his shit in the car. The other fellas were trying to shield their girls from any danger. They each pulled out their guns taking aim. BJ started firing back at the car when it sped off. When they left they made sure everyone was okay, they got in their cars and rolled out. The only thing that went through all of the men heads were who was that shooting at them and why?

Chapter 19

Kim

Kim woke up with a headache the size of Texas. She couldn't remember anything from last night after going to Tracey house and telling them about Quan's rules. Everything else was a blur. She noticed that she had on shorts and a shirt, but she knew she wasn't at her house. As soon as she sat up in the bed, the door opened.

"Damn girl, you finally up?" Jasmine said to Kim.

With one eye open and the other half open Kim said "yeah but I got a mean ass headache though."

Jasmine started to laugh. "You should have more than that. Your ass was past fucked up last night."

"For real? I don't remember anythi... Pause, why am I at your house?" Kim asked just realizing she was at her cousin house.

"You and Quan got in a big fight, so he left the club. Shawn dropped me and you off here." Jasmine informed her.

"What did me and Quan fight about?" Kim asked confused. She knew he was mad but that was just how he been since Shawn came back.

"Girl, you were showing your ass the whole night. You were on the bar dancing to Lil Kim with that short ass dress on, you was drinking like no tomorrow, you told him that y'all were single last night, you sat on Shawn lap right in front of him, and you freaked a lot of the guys in the club." Jasmine went down the list of what Kim's night.

"OMG. I know he is mad. You know I love him I wouldn't hurt him like that." Kim said.

"Oh yeah, I think that why he left because he love you so much. He knocked this nigga out with one punch." Jasmine said.

"What? Quan wouldn't do that. He's always the peace maker."

"Not last night. He was past pissed. His face was red the whole night."

"Damn. Can I get some meds so I can go home?" Kim asked.

Jasmine got up and got Kim some meds for her headache.

"Yo Jaz where is my phone?" Kim asked

"You didn't have it. All you had were your shoes when Shawn found your ass."

"Shit, I didn't drive either. I'm going take a nap to help this hangover. Can you drop me off at home later?" Kim asked.

"Yeah chick." Jasmine said closing the door.

As soon as Kim head hit the pillow she was out like a light.

Quan...

Quan had been up all night just sitting on the couch replaying the whole night in his head. He knew he did wrong towards Kim, but at the time his pride and manhood was too powerful to let him know that he hurt the woman that he loves so much. Another reason he was still up was cause Terence called him last night around 4 telling him that they got shot at while leaving the club. Hearing that pissed him off because he wasn't there, then he found out that Kim left with Shawn and she wasn't home yet. Everything just blocked Quan from thinking straight. He called her cell phone all night over and over and no answer. He wasn't worried about Shawn, he just wanted to make sure Kim was safe.

After sitting there for another hour and realizing that Kim wasn't coming he said "Man fuck this." He jumped up off the couch and ran upstairs to the bedroom. He went in the closet and got his gun and left out the house. His thoughts were all over the place and that day if anybody looked at him funny they were dead. He drove aimless and reckless ending up at his destination in 10minutes top.

He parked the car leaving the keys and door open. He walked up to the door and banged on it as hard as he could.

The person on the other end looked through the peep hole and opened the door. As soon as the door opened, Quan swung a hard right punch across the guy face catching him off guard.

The two men began to fight as if they weren't brothers throwing blow for blow. They both were winded and at the same time they both pulled out their gun aiming it at each other.

"Where the fuck is she?" Quan asked trying to catch his breath, his chest moving up and down.

"Man, you need to calm down. Kim ain't here." Shawn said while lowering his gun.

"Where is she?" Quan asked putting his gun down too.

"She at Jasmine house. I dropped them off last night."

"Oh…" Quan said looking down to the ground as tears fell from his eyes. The only people who ever saw Quan cry was God and now he couldn't hold it back anymore.

"Yo Q, you good? I'm still your brother. You can talk to me whenever you need to. I'm tired of fighting man, we blood." Shawn said.

"Man you know if I knew she was your girl I would have never went after her. This shit is just so much man. This whole situation has me fucked up. I love X like he my son, but he ain't. I want to be selfish and keep him away from you but I can't. I don't want Kim to fall back for you because I fell for that girl hard. I knew she was pregnant and everything but that didn't stop me from loving her. I was there when X was born. When she cried all night because you left her, I was there. Making sure she got out of her depression state I was there. Man this is the hardest decision I ever went though."

Shawn went into his living room and sat on the couch before he started to speak.

"I understand, I wasn't there for her, but that never stopped me from loving her. I even love my son even though he doesn't know who I am. I want to be in my son's life. I love that woman with all of my heart. She is so truthful and caring. She is wife material, but at the same time I see how she looks at you and how when you say little shit to her it hurts her. I know she loves me but she is in love with you." Shawn said, telling his brother the truth.

110

"If she meant that much to you, why did you leave her?" Quan asked.

"It was a leak in our operation that's been handled now. He was setting me up to get a bid, but these weren't any regular cops: They were dirty. They stopped me one day while I was going home and told me all our history. I left to protect you, my mother and Kim. They just knew I had a brother but didn't know your name. They knew my mother but didn't know where she stayed and they knew I had a baby on the way but I kept Kim away from all the workers. So I did it for all of us. That bitch ass cop I'm going to get for threatening my family though."

"Why you ain't let me know?"

"I didn't have time. I couldn't even inform Kim. I had to write her a note." Shawn said.

"Damn. You heard about the shooting?"

"Yeah, I just left. Who do you think it is?" Shawn asked.

"Terence said Kevin and Zoe got in a fight with some niggas." Quan said.

"Yeah we did but they weren't nothing to worry about. We have to have a meeting with the crew because we can't let people bring heat towards us." Shawn said.

"True. I'm about to go find Kim. Peace bro. No more fighting man." Quan said.

"You came over here wildin'." Shawn said giving his brother a hug.

111

"Oh by the way I'm going to tell Kim to bring X over here." Quan said walking out the door to get in his car.

Kim...

Kim woke up 20 minutes later and went to the bathroom. She still had her hangover but she knew she had to get home. She used the spare toothbrushes that she gave her cousin from the dental office she worked at to brush her teeth. After she finished, she changed into some clothes Jasmine left for her. Kim met Jasmine downstairs once she was done and went home.

When Kim walked into the house, it was dark and quiet as if no one was home.

"Quan! Quan!" Kim yelled his name but she got no answer. She went in the kitchen to get some water and headed to her bedroom. Her plans for the day were to sleep the rest of her hangover off. Kim was in a good sleep till she felt someone put their arms around her.

"Hey baby." Kim said.

"Hey baby girl. Were you sleeping well?" Quan asked.

"Yes. I still have a headache but it'll go away." Kim said.

"I was worried about you last night. I called your phone a million times." Quan said.

"I don't know where my phone is. I want to apologize for whatever I did. To be honest I don't remember anything." Kim said turning around to face Quan and looking him in his eyes.

"No you don't have to apologize. I'm sorry for trying to be someone I'm not. I love you, you are my sunshine." Quan said.

Kim loved when he called her his sunshine. She smiled and said, "I love you too, baby."

Kim knew she was madly in love with Quan but in the back of her head she still was in love with Shawn. To get the thoughts out of her head she laid on Quan's chest, listening to his heart beat and went to back to sleep.

Chapter 20

London

London tossed and turned all night long thinking about all the calls she received, the shooting at the club, and crazy feeling that she felt as she go places as if somebody is following her. She was having a hard time sleeping. When she finally went to sleep, her alarm clock went off letting her know it was time to get up for work. Sleepy from tossing and turning all night she pulled herself out of the bed. She was moving slower than she ever had.

"You going to be late." BJ said as he sat up in the bed and looked at London getting dressed.

Busy getting dressed she said "I know, I'm trying to hurry up. You are going to have to take Bryant to day care."

"So are you going to pick him up if I drop him off?" BJ asked.

"I guess Brandon." London said.

"I got you ma, calm down." BJ said getting up and going to Bryant's room to get him dressed.

London finished getting dressed and gave the men in her life a kiss, then ran out the door. She was driving fast to make it to work on time.

She made it to work right on time with no minutes or seconds to spare. Monday's were always her busy days. She had back to back meetings and proposals due.

While she was in the middle of working her office phone rang.

"This is London Smith." London said.

"Hey sis. What you doing?" Lorren said.

"Hey Lorren, I'm working." London said laughing a little because that was a silly question.

"Oh I called you because I didn't talk to you yesterday. I wanted to let you know who was at the party."

"Who?" London asked still typing on her computer.

"Mat." Lorren said.

"Who? Matthew Parker?" London stopped typing and asked.

"Yes girl." Lorren said.

"I ain't seen Mat in 8 years." London said.

"Yeah, he looks so good too." Lorren said.

"Yeah I bet. You know he always told me you would be his wife." London told her sister.

"Girl, you are silly, I'm about to let you go back to work."

"It's my lunch break right now. Talk to you later sis." London said getting off the phone with Lorren.

London finished typing up her proposal and she got up to go get something to eat. Deciding to get some subway which was down the street from her office, she walked outside. As she walked she began to get the feeling that she was being followed so she pulled out her cell phone and called someone she knew who made her feel safe.

"Hello?" BJ said half sleep.

"I know your butt ain't still sleep." London said to BJ.

"Naw, I was resting my eyes. What's up beautiful?" BJ asked checking his phone.

"Nothing just wanted to talk while I go get some food."

"Oh ok so you using me?" BJ asked now watching ESPN.

"Yeah, you can say that." London told BJ in between laughing.

"That's cool. What you about to get for lunch?"

"Subway. Oh so while you on the phone, what you want to eat for dinner?"

"I want steak and some other shit." BJ said all up in the recap of the basketball game he missed.

"That's helping me a lot." London said knowing he wasn't paying attention.

"Ma, get some veggies and rice or potatoes or both. I don't know."

"That's fine. I'll pick up whatever I see." London said getting aggravated.

"That's fine with me. You know I would eat whatever you cook." BJ said making some humor out of London frustration.

"I know you would fat boy." London said.

"So, you got jokes. You know this is all muscle." BJ said flexing his muscles as if London could see him.

"Yeah whatever muscle man. Oh by the way you have to pick Bryant up."

"I can't, I have to hit the streets." BJ said.

"I know but I have to work a little late and I have to go to the grocery store."

"Iight he can chill with me." BJ said not wanting to hear London whine.

"Don't have my son on the block either." London said sternly.

"Yeah iight."

"Look fat boy I'm at the subway now. I'll talk to you later."

"Later spoiled brat. Love you."

"Love you too." London said hanging up.

London got her food and grabbed a seat. She was texting her friends and eating, when a text came to her phone. It read:

"You can't run from me. I am everywhere. I want you back London and I won't stop till I have you."

London read the text message and got spooked. She didn't know what to do. She looked around and she didn't notice anybody that looked familiar. Grabbing her stuff, she headed back to the office quickly.

She was scared but then her mind went to ease when she started to do some work. She was so focused on her work that she didn't notice she was supposed to get off an hour ago. She got her stuff together and headed out the door so she can make it to the grocery store.

When she got to the grocery store it wasn't crowded which made her happy. She grabbed all the stuff she needed for dinner and got some stuff for Bryant to snack on. After she got everything she headed to her car. London was busy putting the groceries in the trunk when she heard the voice that makes her skin crawl. She turned around and noticed Keith.

"What do you want Keith?" London asked loosening up the mace on her keychain.

"I wanted to see you London." Keith said walking closer to London.

"How you know where I was at?" London said getting scared.

"I'm a computer engineer, I know everything." Keith said walking closer to her.

"I'm going to need you to stop calling and texting my phone."

"Or what's going to happen?" Keith said not liking the fact that London was getting loud on him.

"I'm going to have…" London couldn't even finish what she was going to say before Keith grabbed her by the neck.

"You going to have your boyfriend come and get me? Because of you I lost everything. My family doesn't want to be around *me, I lost my job and then you don't want to come back to me." Keith's light skin face was now red. His cornrows were messy. He looked like a crazy person. "If I can't have you no one will." Keith said still holding London by the neck and squeezing it.

London took the mace and sprayed it in his eyes. He was blinded so he let go and she kicked him in his groin. While Keith dropped to the ground immediately, she hopped in her car and sped off while tears rolled down her face. She was so shaken up that she couldn't stop her hand from shaking so she could call anyone. She pulled in her driveway; she jumped out of the car and ran to the house leaving everything behind.

As soon as she opened the door, BJ was walking out of the kitchen going to the living room. With tears running down her face she ran into BJ arms. BJ didn't notice that she was crying till he felt his shirt wet.

"What's wrong baby?" BJ asked pulling her back so he could see her face.

"He chocked me." London said, crying hysterically.

"Who chocked you?" BJ asked not understanding what happened.

While BJ tried to get info out of London, Bryant came running towards his parents. "Mommy"

"Little man let me talk to your mom right quick." BJ said making sure Bryant went upstairs.

London told him everything. BJ was pissed off because he wasn't there to protect her and if something would have happened to her he would have been mad at his self.

"Look, I'm going to get you a new phone. I'm going to take you to work and stuff from now on. Do you understand?"

"Yes." London said lying on the couch.

BJ went outside to get the groceries and call his boys to let them know what the deal was. BJ knew he had to do something to that punk ass nigga before his wifey got hurt.

BJ took care of London that night. He cooked and made sure she put something on her neck because there were finger prints on it and made sure that Bryant was good. When everyone in his house was sleep, BJ left to go and pass word on the street. He wanted Keith alive.

Chapter 21

Lorren

Lorren sat up late flicking the channels on her TV. For some reason she couldn't sleep. Rico was gone, and the kids were sleep. She hadn't been able to sleep for awhile now. She was either worried about Rico or having crazy dreams about Mat. A secret that Lorren kept from everyone, even her sister, was that Mat was her first. She never knew how to tell her sister because she was always judgmental and she damn sure wasn't going to tell Rico that Mat was her first. He would kill Mat for sure. Lorren needed to talk to someone just to get it off her chest. So she decided to call Danni.

After five rings Danni answered.

"Hey Danni. Were you sleep?" Lorren asked already knowing that she was sleep since it was 3:30 am.

"Naw Lorren, I was up dancing." Danni said sarcastically.

"Yeah, well keep the party going." Lorren said.

"What's up Lorren? I do have to go to work in the morning."

"I can't sleep and I need to talk to someone." Lorren said.

"Out of all people you called me? You know Kim stay up late, India always willing to talk, London your twin you ain't call her." Danni said knowing something was wrong.

"I didn't call any of them because I know you would give me good advice and everybody else is going through their own mess."

"I'm sorry Lorren, What's going on?"

"I've been keeping a secret from London and Rico." Lorren said pausing trying to get her thoughts together.

"What is it?" Danni asked

"Well, you know how everyone thinks that Rico was my first: he wasn't. It was this dude name Matthew. London and I grew up with him. He got locked up and after he got locked up I started messing with Rico. That's when I lied to Rico telling him I never had sex before and everything." Lorren said.

"So, that is your past. If you kept it a secret this long you can keep it that way." Danni said.

"Yeah but I keep having dreams about him. Then to make matters worse I ran into him at Kevin's birthday party and I can't get him out of my head. I just feel guilty. I feel like I'm cheating on Rico."

"Well, this is what you need to do. Confront Matthew and see if there are feelings there and if not you are good. The reason that you are having those dreams is because you're thinking about the past, wondering about the "what ifs". Talk to Mat as a friend. Afterwards try and keep it on that level. You know Rico's crazy ass doesn't play." Danni said.

"Thanks Danni, I needed to hear that. You can go to sleep now." Lorren said as she hung up the phone.

Lorren took what Danni said into consideration and called Mat. The phone rang three times but to Lorren it felt as if it was ringing forever.

"Hello" Mat said sounding fully awake.

"Hey Mat, this is Lorren."

"I know who it is. Your name came up." Mat said with a little chuckle.

"Oh," Lorren said trying to think of what she was going to say next. It was a brief silence.

"So what do I owe this call?" Mat asked.

"Well I never told anyone about our love affair and lately I've been having dreams about you." Lorren began.

"They just dreams Lorren." Mat said laughing.

"I know but I feel like I'm cheating on my man. I don't know if seeing you brought back old feelings or not but I feel the only way to get rid of these dreams and things is to ask you if you would like to go out. That way I can see if the feelings are still there." Lorren said.

"This is crazy but sure I'll take you out. When would you like to go out?" Mat asked.

"How does Thursday night sound? My man is kind of crazy so I would meet you where ever you pick." Lorren said just thinking about Rico's reaction.

"Thursday is fine and don't worry about your man. I'll call you later with more details." Mat said.

"Ok cool. Good night." Lorren said hanging up.

After getting off the phone with Mat she felt a little relief. She dozed straight off and was sleeping well. When her sleep starting to get deep, she began to dream.

"Mat, take me right here." Lorren said as soon as she seen Mat walk up to her car.

Mat pulled Lorren out of the car and put her on the hood, stepping between her legs in the process. She must have known she was going to get some dick because she wore a skirt for easy access. He hiked her skirt up and while kissing on her neck, entered two fingers inside of her. While he let kisses trail down her neck, he added pressure to her clit, making her reach her climax quickly. After making her come, he knew it was time to replace his fingers with his dick. Unbuckling his pants and lowering his boxers, he entered her in one swift movement. He was fucking her the same way she remembered. Lorren was feeling herself climax again.

Before she could climax, she heard her name being called by a voice that wasn't Mat's. Lorren opened her eyes and noticed that Rico was home.

"Damn girl was you having a bad dream? Your ass was all over the bed." Rico said as he took his clothes off.

Lorren just looked at him because she didn't know what to say. Only did he not know she wasn't having a bad dream; she was having the dream of her life.

Lorren finally broke out of her train of thought and said "Naw, I just couldn't sleep so I guess I was tossing and turning."

124

"Oh well a nigga tired so keep yourself on your side." Rico said jokingly while pulling her in his arms.

Lorren took a deep breath and went to sleep in Rico's arms praying that she won't dream about Mat and that Danni's plan works.

Chapter 22

Danni

Danni had been so nervous of doing anything now ever since the crooked cops came to her job. She was nervous because they knew so much about her and she didn't know when they would come back to her job and embarrass her again.

Danni made her way to work, tired from being woken up by Lorren who needed her advice. All she wanted to do was go to work, come home and relax. Little did she know was that her day was about to get extra interesting. She went into work and of course talked to Jaden, who informed her that some girl came into the office and personally asked for her. Danni was puzzled by who would come into the doctor's office and ask for her to exam them. She knew it wasn't any of her friends because they would have called her that night or morning and told her to make them an appointment.

"Jaden who was the girl?" Danni asked.

"Girl, I have no idea who she was. She was kind of ghetto and loud." Jaden said sucking his teeth.

"How in the hell she know me?" Danni asked getting nervous.

"I have no idea honey. I do have her name though because she said she would come back at 1." Jaden informed Danni.

"When were you going to tell me you had a name?" Danni asked play hitting Jaden.

"Now bitch. Her name is Toni Adams."

126

"Toni Adams? Why the hell was she looking for me?" Danni asked.

"Well, maybe she needs a look down there." Jaden said while laughing.

Jaden and Danni went their separate ways since it was a busy day at the doctor's office. They couldn't wait till 12 o'clock to come. They just wanted to be as far away from the office as possible. Jaden and Danni went to Chipotle to get some lunch and eat inside. While they ate they talked about everything and everybody. They noticed they had 10 minutes to get back to work so they wrapped up their leftover food and left. When they walked back into the office, their adviser told them which room they told their patients to go in.

When Danni walked into her exam room and saw Toni Adams sitting on the bed, you could have bought Danni for a penny.

"Hey Danielle" Toni said.

"How you doing Toni?" Danni asked.

Toni was Danni's friend from college and also Bryon's cousin. The other girls didn't really care for Toni but Danni always was her friend, which was how Danni met Bryon. They were cool, but Toni was bipolar and kind of crazy, and to add on top of that she took meds. With Toni you never knew what her mood was. She had stopped being Danni's friend because Danni was hanging with her girls more and limiting her time around Toni. She couldn't take the mood swings and she got word that Toni use to lace her weed, so when Danni found that out she told Bryon and Toni didn't like that she told him about her life at college. Danni was only looking out for Toni but Toni didn't see it like that. She just felt Danni was a back stabbing bitch. Even when Danni would go to Bryon's family functions, Toni would never show because she knew how serious Danni and Bryon were. It had been 7 years since Danni saw Toni, let alone spoke to her. Danni was thinking what she wants now.

"I'm good, I just took a home pregnancy test and it said positive." Toni said.

"Ok, so I'm going to take a look and let you know how far a long you are." Danni said.

While Danni was examining her, Toni wanted to know some information, so she began to ask Danni questions.

"So, I see you doing good after college." Toni said.

"Yeah, I'm doing what I wanted to do with my life." Danni said wondering what she wanted.

"So you have any children?"

"Yeah I have one boy."

"So you have a child, which means you must be talking to someone serious?" Toni stated but more like a question.

"Yes, I have a wonderful man that I love." Danni said getting up to wash her hands.

"How is everybody?"

"Everybody is great. Ok from the reading, it looks like you are 8 weeks. You'll have to schedule another appointment so you can get a follow up." Danni said trying to get Toni out of there quick. She was asking too many questions.

"Oh Ok. I wanted to know did you want to hang out today. I wanted to talk to you more and everything. You know, play catch up a bit." Toni asked as she got up off the table.

"Umm well, I was going to hang with Kim, but I'm sure you could come along." Danni said.

"Ok, cool so what's your number?" Toni asked pulling out her cell phone.

Danni was a little nervous to give it to her but they exchanged numbers. The whole day Danni just wanted to know what she wanted.

As soon as she got in her car, she picked up her phone and dialed Kim with the quickness.

"Hello." Kim said.

"What you doing Kim?"

"Just leaving work about to go pick Xavier up from school. Then we going to Chuck E Cheese today. What's up?"

"Well I need you to do me a favor. Oh and you'll never guess who came in the office today?"

"Who and what is the favor?" Kim asked knowing something was up.

"Toni Adams and the favor is can…" Danni couldn't even finish her sentence before Kim cut her off.

"Toni Adams, Bryon crazy ass cousin. You better not ask me to hang with y'all two either. I love you to death Danni but I don't like that bitch." Kim said.

"Come on Kim, I would do it for you." Danni asked.

"Danni open your eyes. The only time she come around is when she need something or want something. That bitch is just crazy."

"I know Kim, that's why I want you to go with me. You can read people fast and you would know what their intentions are." Danni said.

"Alright I'll go but we are going to chuck E cheese because I promise my baby we would go and you owe me Red Lobster." Kim said.

"That's cool. Thanks Boo!" Danni said, and then hung up the phone.

After picking Genesis up, Danni told Toni they were going to Chuck E Cheese. She went home and changed her clothes since they were meeting at 5pm. Leaving out shortly after, Kim and Danni got there at the same time and went inside to get a table while they waited for Toni to show up.

"I can't believe you got me out here hanging with Miss bipolar herself." Kim said as they went and got tokens and pizza for the boys.

"She was cool in the office maybe she changed since college." Danni said shrugging.

"I hope so. I hope she just wanted to apologize or some shit to you for getting mad at you when you didn't want to hit her lace weed and shit." Kim said.

Danni just thought about all of the drama and shit she went through with Toni, who she called her friend but a couple of turn downs and Toni started to bad talk Danni and everything.

While they gave the boys tokens and waited for the pizza to come to the table, they just had regular conversation and then they notice a lady with three children walk up to the table. It was Toni.

"Hey y'all sorry I'm late but Rob Jr. didn't want to come but he had no choice." Toni said.

Toni had Rob Jr. when they were in undergrad. He was 9 years old now, Gina was 7 and James was 5 and now she was pregnant again. The kids were bad too. They were begging for tokens and Toni didn't buy them any, so Kim and Danni brought the kids some tokens so they could play.

"Damn Toni you were busy making babies." Kim said. Kim really didn't care for Toni because she didn't like how she carried herself and she was a foul person.

"Yeah, I guess." Toni said. She didn't care for Kim either. She felt Kim was a bitch who thought she was better than everybody else.

"So what you do after college?" Kim asked. She was trying to feel Toni out.

"I haven't had time to go back to school but I plan on though. I have been living." Toni said smacking her lips together.

"So, where is your children's father?" Danni asked curiously.

"Oh well as you know they all have different daddies, but the one that I am currently with he just got locked up." Toni said like it was nothing.

"Oh wow. So what did you need to ask me? You said you had something to ask me when we were at the office." Danni asked.

As soon as Toni was about to answer the pizza arrived, along with the kids running for the pizza. The kids tore the pizza and salad up. When they finished eating they got back up and finished playing games.

Kim wanted to know what the answer was to Danni's question so she asked Toni "So what you wanted to ask Danni?"

Toni just looked at Kim then said "I'm kind of behind on my rent and about to get kicked out and I wanted to know could you lend me the money or let me stay with you until I find another place. Since we are like family, you were my friend and dating my favorite cousin."

Kim and Danni looked at each other as if to say "this bitch is crazy". Danni didn't know what to say. Kim on the other hand took her phone out to text Danni real quick.

"That bitch is lying because she is on welfare which means her rent is $20 a month. She going to get in your house and leave them damn kids."

Danni read the text and realized that Kim had a point. So she had to be quick.

"What do me dating your cousin have to do with you asking for money or a place to stay. Toni tell me the truth. How much is your rent?" Danni asked.

132

"Well, I know you were dating my cousin and I know he left you something, his house or something and my rent is $580." Toni said.

"Well, I left Bryon way before he passed so I don't have anything that deals with him. As for lending you money or offering my house for you to stay I have to talk to my husband." Danni said.

"Come on Danni, you can call him and ask him if it's ok for us to stay for a couple of days?"

"Are you on that stuff?" Kim asked because she was getting drug addict tease from her.

"Look bitch ain't anybody talking to you." Toni snapped at Kim.

Kim just looked at Toni and was about to say something but Danni jumped in and said "I'm going to have to get back with you on that Toni."

Toni jumped up from the table and said "You still the same stuck up bitch hanging with them dumb ass hoes as friends. You only think about your damn self. Fuck you bitch and the bitches you hang with."

After she said that she snatched her kids up and stormed out of the chuck E cheese.

"Well, that was a great evening." Kim said laughing.

"I never got cursed out that bad before." Danni said laughing along with Kim.

"Well, I guess I'm a hoe and a bitch." Kim said.

133

"I see ain't shit change from college."

"But on the real she on drugs."

"I know."

They let the little men have a little more fun before heading their own ways home.

Chapter 23

India

India had a long day at work today. She had to go to the police department and gather some information about an upcoming case she has.

"Shit" India said out loud.

"What's wrong with you?" Kevin asked with his eyes still closed.

"Kevin please tell me you turned the alarm clock on." India said as she got out of bed.

"Yeah, I set it for 6:00" Kevin said.

Kevin went out last night and was high and tipsy. When he walked in the room he had tripped and unplugged the clock. He picked it up and set the clock back.

India had a feeling that he did something stupid, so she walked over to the clock, and then she said "Fool you set the clock for 6 pm."

"Oh damn, my bad ma." Kevin said as he turned over and pulled the covers over his head.

"Your bad! Thanks a lot to you nigga I'm going to be late for work." India said getting her clothes out. While talking to Kevin, she realized that he had went back to sleep on her. So walking to the bathroom she slapped him upside his head and headed to the shower.

After taking her shower she walked back into the bedroom to see that Kevin was all over the bed.

"Kevin" India yelled.

"What?" He said trying to sleep.

"You have to get up and take the twins to school." India said putting on her clothes.

"Yo I'm tired. Why you can't take them."

"I would take them but some dumb asshole set the clock wrong, making me late for work."

"Iight to shut you up, I'll take them." Kevin said pulling a pillow over his head.

"They are your kids too. They going to be late if you don't get up" India said grabbing her heels.

Kevin didn't respond, so she walked over to him and applied pressure to the pillow which was on his head.

"Get up." She said before she walked out the door.

India was driving fast so she could make it to work. When she got there, she was 30 minutes late. She went straight to working on her case. Before she knew it, it was time for her to go pass the police station and meet her new client.

When she arrived at the police station it was crowded so she walked to the front desk.

"Hello I am India Scott and I am here to get the information on my client Jason Turner." India said to the woman behind the desk.

"Yes Ms. Scott, you could go to the second office on the left and Mr. Jones would help you."

India walked into the office and saw a very attractive officer. Before she knew what she was doing, she was licking her lips and looking him up and down as if she could see him in her bed. She was looking at his lips which looked like they could do amazing damage to a pussy.

She cleared her throat and said "Hi, I am India Scott."

The officer looked up from his papers and smiled, "Oh yeah, you here for the Turner file. I haven't had enough time to get the file ready, but if you give me a few I could have it together."

India thought to herself *"he might be sexy as fuck, but why niggas never have shit ready."*

"Sure I can wait." India said with a smile.

After 10 minutes, India was bored just sitting there waiting for Officer Jones, so she picked up her phone and called Kevin.

"Yeah." Kevin said when he picked up.

"Did you take the kids to school?" India asked. While looking through the door at Officer Jones, as he talked to some girl.

"Naw, I went back to sleep. They right here watching TV." Kevin said

"Kevin you know they not supposed to miss school. What is wrong with you?"

"Look ma, it's cool. Like you said earlier these are my kids too."

"Yeah whatever. I have to go." India said while she noticed Officer Jones coming back to the office.

India was mad at Kevin for being irresponsible.

"Here go the file, Ms. Scott."

"Thank you." India said as she looked through the file to make sure everything was correct.

"So is there anything else I can help you with?" this time Officer Jones was flirting with her.

"Oh that'll be all." India said getting up to leave.

"You sure?" Officer Jones asked again this time grabbing his dick and licking his lips at India.

India looked at him getting hard and had to think about her dumb ass baby father and her children.

"Thanks for the offer, but that will be it." India said leaving.

India had to get her head together after witnessing the officer's dick getting hard. Not paying attention she ran into someone.

"Oh my bad." She said then noticed who she ran into. "Toni?"

"Oh hey India, long time no hear." Toni said.

"Yeah I know. What do you work here?" India asked figuring it was weird that she was just hanging in the police station.

"Girl no I just needed some help."

"Oh ok. Well see you around. I have to go." India said. She couldn't be around Toni too long. She didn't know when her mood would change.

India had to spread the news about who she just ran into and called Danni.

"Hello?" Danni asked in a whisper.

"Bitch why you whispering? What the fuck are you doing?"

"I left out the examination room. I'm in the middle of an appointment with a wolf pussy. What's up?" Danni asked.

"Bitch you are stupid. Girl guess who I just ran into."

"Who, and hurry up I have to get back to work." Danni said.

"Toni, Bryon crazy cousin." India yelled.

"Small world, she came in yesterday." Danni said checking her nails.

"Damn what happened? What she want?" India asked.

"Bitch I can't talk right now, what I tell you I was doing?" Danni said.

"Iight you gay bitch, call me when you get off." India laughed.

When she got off the phone she headed to see her client and waited for Danni to hit her back. She knew Toni was a show

139

and wanted to know why she all of a sudden starting showing her face again. What was the catch?

Chapter 24

What do you want me to do?

Officer Jones walked in his house, all he smelt was
beans and hot dogs, and heard kids running around yelling. Drew
Jones was 26 years old and took his job serious. He loved being
a police officer and no one or anybody would come between him
and his job. A month ago when he was placed on the case of
Bryon Miller he knew this wasn't going to be an easy one to
break because whoever murdered him did a good job making it
so that wasn't found until a year later. So when Bryon's funeral
arrived and he noticed how bad his so call fiancé talked about
him, he knew off the back who to follow and keep tabs on. After
the funeral he ran into one of Bryon's cousin and they began to
talk. When he started talking to her she never mentioned that she
had children. When she asked can she stay with him for awhile,
he extended the offer, and to add on that she was a good fuck.
After staying with him for 3 days, she introduced her kids to
him, and they've been staying there ever since. The only reason
he let Toni stay with him is because she told him she was
pregnant and he needed her help with the case.

"Toni what is that damn smell?" Drew asked annoyed.
As he walked through to the kitchen, he saw all of the kids at the
table and noticed that his house was a mess.

"It's food." Toni said. "Do you want some?"

"Naw, I'm good. Clean up my house though. Looks like
a bunch of pigs live here."

"I'm going to clean up your house damn." Toni said
rolling her eyes.

"Did you do what I asked you to do?" Drew asked walking to the room as Toni trailed behind him. He couldn't stand looking at her. He couldn't wait for her to get the information that he needed.

"I went and saw her. She brought her bitch of a friend so I couldn't get any information out of her." Toni said.

"That's not what I want to hear. You need to try harder or you and your kids are out of here." Drew said sitting on the bed taking off his shoes.

"So you just going to put me the mother of your child out, on the street." Toni asked looking at him.

"Don't play me, you know that's not my baby." Drew said.

"What do you want me to do? I'm trying but she isn't trying to give up any information."

"First, I want you to suck this dick. Second, I want you to get your ass on that cell phone and call that bitch." Drew said while unzipping his pants.

Toni got on her knees and began to suck Drew dick. Toni had skills sucking dick, but Drew didn't respect her so he fucked her face then came in her mouth, forcing her to swallow is cum. When she was done he looked at her and got up from the bed.

"Now do what the fuck I told you to do, before you find yourself homeless." Drew said.

Toni just looked at him and knew what she had to do.

Falling for a
Drug Dealer

Part IV

IT ALL COMES
TO AN END

Chapter 25

Lisa

Lisa paced back and forth waiting for the bitch Shermika to bring the baby so she could see if it was Terence's or not. She had it up to the crown of her head messing with that damn girl. She swore to herself if it comes out to be Terence baby she would leave him just because that bitch would have to be in their life.

"Yo Lisa, what's wrong baby?" Terence asked when he walked in the living room.

Lisa who was still in her train of thought and wasn't paying Terence any attention kept walking back and forth.

"Lisa." He said louder so that she can snap out of her trance.

"Oh, what's up hun?" Lisa asked.

"The phone is for you." Terence handed her the phone while still looking at her crazy.

Lisa didn't pay his looks any mind.

"Hello" Lisa said into the phone.

"What up fool? What you doing?" Kim asked.

"Shit. Just waiting." Lisa said.

"Well, do you want to go to the gym with me after you finish waiting?" Kim asked, not having a clue what Lisa was waiting for.

"Naw, not today. I got mad business to handle. I'll try tomorrow." Lisa said still walking.

"Ok cool. By the way what are you waiting on?" Kim asked.

When Lisa was about to answer Kim's question the door bell rung.

"Kim I have to go. I'll talk to you later." Lisa hung up the phone before anymore questions were asked.

Lisa got to the door before Terence could. She opened it with no smile or anything on her face. Even though she told Shermika to bring the baby over so they could do a DNA test and everything she wanted to beat her ass.

"Well, can I come in?" Shermika asked holding her daughter hand.

"Sure." Lisa stepped to the side and allowed them to come in.

Lisa just looked at the little girl. She was so pretty. She had light brown eyes, a smooth brown complexion and very pretty hair. She could have passed for Terence child. She looked like she could be TJ sister.

Terence came into the living room where Lisa, Shermika, and the baby girl were at.

"This is Tasha. Tasha this is your daddy." Shermika introduced Tasha to Terence.

"Please stop saying that." Terence said then walked over to the little girl.

"Hey lil mama, what's your name?" Terence asked the little girl.

"Tasha." She said in a shy voice.

Terence looked at Lisa then Shermika and said "iight, I got this you can leave." He said to Shermika.

"Do I have to come and pick her up?" Shermika asked with an attitude.

"Naw, I'll drop her off." Terence said.

"Yes, WE'LL drop her off." Lisa added.

Shermika got up and gave her daughter a kiss and headed out the door.

"Are you hungry sweetheart?" Lisa asked, squatting down to look at the little girl.

"Yes." Tasha said quietly.

"What would you like to eat?"

"I don't know." Tasha said.

"Well, let's go find something." Lisa grabbed Tasha's hand and headed to the kitchen. When they were in the kitchen,

Lisa made a sandwich for TJ and Tasha. As they ate and the kids talked to each other, Lisa just looked and wondered how she would act if the child is Terence. She wouldn't dare treat a child bad. While she was in a trance, Terence walked up behind her.

"What you thinking about?"

"Nothing." Lisa said

"Why you lying?" Terence asked.

"I'm not lying." Lisa couldn't lie to save her life.

"I know what you thinking and she is not my daughter." Terence informed Lisa then gave her a kiss on her forehead.

They enjoyed the company of the children playing around. Terence and Lisa were getting used to Tasha being around, but they had to do what they had to do. Terence had ordered a home DNA test. Around dinner time Terence took the test. They had to send it back to the lab and know the results in a week.

"So Tasha tell me about yourself." Terence asked.

"My mommy said I will be living with my daddy soon." Tasha said.

"Did your mother tell you who your daddy is?" Terence asked.

"She said you, but I go over my other daddy house after school."

After what Tasha had said, Lisa knew that Shermika was playing Terence for a fool. Either she wanted money out of him or she wanted to be with him. Either way, Lisa was going to make sure that shit didn't happen.

"Oh ok. Are you ready to go home?" Terence asked.

"Yes." Tasha replied shyly, getting down from the couch.

Lisa, Terence, TJ and Tasha were in the car heading to Shermika house. When they pulled up they saw this light skin dude on Shermika porch talking to her.

"You lying ass bitch. I was taking care of that damn girl for three years and now I find out she ain't my child. I should fuck you up."

"She is your daughter." Shermika said crying.

"Well, why the fuck is she with some other nigga now. I come over here and see my damn daughter but you sitting here telling me she with some other nigga."

"I am not sure who the father is. I believe she is yours though."

"Yeah we'll see. Imma get a DNA test bitch. So help me God if that little girl ain't mines, I'm splitting your shit on sight."

Terence and Lisa sat in the car listening to the conversation. Tasha looked up and said "That's my daddy." Unbuckling herself from her seat and opening her door, she ran to the porch where Sherkmika was crying.

"Daddy, daddy." Tasha yelled while she ran up on the porch.

The light skin dude looked down at her and picked her up.

"What's up baby girl? Where your trick ass mom have you at?"

"I went to my other daddy house." Tasha said playing with his shirt.

Terence got out of the car and walked over to the light skin dude.

"My name is Terence and I know this is not my daughter but to keep Shermika ass off my back me and my wife arranged an outing so that we could find out. We took a DNA test and when it comes back negative that bitch up there can never bother me again. You feel me partner?" Terence asked.

"Yeah, I feel you son. I can't wait to get this DNA so I can get full custody of my daughter because she ain't shit but a slick ass trick." The light skin dude said looking at Shermika while speaking to Terence.

Shermika just stood on the porch looking dumb as the two men who she thought were her daughter's father talked bad about her.

When Terence got in the car Lisa looked at him and said "It's not over between me and that chick."

Terence could say nothing because he knew that Lisa was serious and was going to do something about it.

Chapter 26

Tracey

Tracey was at work when she got the best news ever. Before she graduated, she had applied to work in San Diego, CA at this private school, but they told her that they didn't have any openings but if any came about they would contact her. It had been so many years that Tracey had forgot about the school in San Diego until they called her while she was in class. They informed her how much she would get paid, they were willing to pay for her relocation fees and any other fees she would have for her trip out there. They really wanted Tracey to work with them. She informed them that she had to run it by her boyfriend. They understood and gave her 2 months to let them know.

First thing Tracey did was send an email to all her friends telling them they need to meet up that afternoon at a local soul food restaurant. Then she had to find a way to tell Zoe.

After work Tracey asked her brother Tone to go pick Handsome up for her. When she pulled up at the soul food restaurant she walked in and sat at a table waiting for her friends to show up.

"What up bitch." India said when she walked in and saw Tracey sitting at a table in the front.

"Nothing hoe. Where the hell is everybody?" Tracey said.

"Well, Danni is parking. Lisa, Lorren and London are on their way. Kim….I haven't talked to her." India said.

"What it do people?" Danni said walking up to the table smiling.

About five minutes later everyone but Kim walked in. While everyone was finally seated, Kim walked over to the table with Xavier.

"Sorry y'all but I had to bring him. It was late notice and I couldn't find Quan." Kim said as she walked to the table.

"That's cool. I have something to talk to y'all about." Tracey said. Before she could continue the waiter came over and took their order.

"So what you have to talk to us about Tracey?" Lisa asked.

"Well, you guys know how I always wanted to teach at a private school. Well I got a call today and they said that I have a job."

All of the girls were excited and proud of Tracey.

"That's not the rest of it. The job is in San Diego, CA." Tracey said.

All of the smiles disappeared and the table became quiet.

"What you mean in San Diego? You just are going to leave us." Kim asked.

"Kim you can't be mad at her. She just following her dreams." Lisa said.

The girls started to fuss and talk over each other, trying to give their opinion on the matter at hand.

"Look you guys, I'm not sure if I'm going to take the job. All of my family is here and I don't know how I would manage out there." Tracey said truthfully.

151

"I'm sorry Tracey and if that is your dream then I think you should go. At least that gives us a place to visit." Kim said.

"Thanks Kim." Tracey said.

The girls enjoyed their dinner and parted ways when they were done. Tracey was happy that she had her friends vote, but now she had to break it to her dad and brothers.

"Hey dad." Tracey said when she walked in the house.

"Hey sweetie, your bad ass son is somewhere around this house."

"I have something to talk to you about."

Her father immediately became anxious, "Are you ok? Is everything ok?"

"Yes daddy everything is ok." Tracey reassured him.

"Well, what's the problem?"

"Well, I was offered a job in San Diego and I just wanted to run it by you."

"That is wonderful. I am so proud of you." Tracey's father said smiling at his only daughter.

"Thank you dad. I knew you would support me. How do you think Zoe is going to take this?"

"Don't worry about how he takes it; only thing that matters is that you are happy sweetie." Tracey's father said then kissed her on the forehead.

Tracey talked to her father for a little while then decided to head home.

When Tracey made it home she gave Handsome a bath and he was sleep right after that. She got herself ready for the next work day when Zoe walked in the house.

"Hey big head." Zoe said as he gave her a kiss.

"Hey fool."

"How was your day?" Zoe asked while pulling off his clothes.

"It was good. I got a question to ask you."

"That's good. What's the question?"

"How would you feel about relocating?" Tracey asked.

"I don't know. Why you ask that question?" Zoe asked.

"I was offered a job in San Diego, CA." Tracey said speedily.

"Well, I hope you told them you won't be taking it." Zoe said.

"This is the type of job I've been waiting for my whole life."

"You iight, I already told you, you don't have to work."

"What would happen if I tell you I am going to take the job?" Tracey said.

"If you take the job you are going by yourself. My son will stay here with me." Zoe said.

"So you just gonna to be selfish." Tracey said.

"You the one trynna to take my son away from me and you call me selfish. Look you ain't taking that job so that's it and I don't want to hear anything else about it. I'm going to sleep in the guest room." Zoe said leaving out of the bedroom with a sad looking Tracey still standing by the bed.

Chapter 27

India

India sat at her office desk talking to her cousin Peaches while looking over some files. She and Peaches made plans to go clubbing all weekend. India was tired of being in the house on weekends and messing around with her damn friends she was going to be big as a house with how much they ate out. It was a Friday that she was waiting for. She knew that Kevin and them had a business trip, so she wanted the weekend to be full of fun with her girls since all the men were busy handling business. India already made plans for her parents to watch the twins.

She got off the phone with Peaches; and called Lorren, London, Tracey, Kim, Danni, and Lisa. They agreed to go out Friday but they didn't know about Saturday, each of them had their different reasons.

As soon as India got home she packed the twins bags and took them to her parents' house. When she was leaving out of her parents' house she kissed her kids and gave her parents a kiss. "Thanks ma and dad." Once she said that she hopped in the car and headed home fast. She had to think of an outfit, so when she finally got home, she raced upstairs and tore through her closet. While searching through her dresses her phone began to ring. Looking down at the screen she saw Kevin was calling her.

"Hello?" India said.

"What up baby?" Kevin said.

"Ain't shit baby what's up?" India said holding the phone to her ear while still going through her dress options.

"Same ole same ole. What you doing?"

"About to go out to the club, so I'm looking through the closet for something to wear." India said.

"Who said you can go out?" Kevin asked with bass in his voice.

"I said I can go out. You got a problem with that?" India asked with attitude.

"Yeah, I do. You don't go to the club when I'm at home so what's the difference now."

"Look I want to go out when you home but you just be bitching." India said pulling out her dress for the night. She looked it over and knew that she would turn heads with the plunging neckline and mesh sides.

"Yo India don't make me have to come home and fuck you up. You think I'm playing with your ass. You wait till I see you."

"Look Kevin you messing up my vibe, so I'm about to hang up now. I love you, bye." India said hanging up on Kevin before he can say anything else.

Around 11, all of the girls were ready. Kim and India were driving that night. The girls went to club "Passion". They all were ready to party and live the single life if only for one night.

"Bitches I am so happy y'all came out with me." India said sipping on a drink while sitting in the VIP section.

"Aw man you being gay dawg." Kim said with a glass in her hand.

All of the girls started to laugh with Kim. Needing to scope the scene out, the girls went to the dance floor. They were dancing and partying the night away. When they finally decided to leave the dance floor, the lights started to flicker on. That let them know that it was close to closing time. The girls didn't want to go home as of yet, so they opted to hit up Ihop since it was always the move after the club. They all ended up staying at India's house because they were having fun like they were still in college. When they woke up, the girls ended up going their separate ways to do their Saturday errands. India looked at her cell phone, and then at the phone caller id and noticed that Kevin had been calling the phone back to back. Before India went to the club she left her cell phone at home on purpose.

She picked up the house phone and dialed Kevin number.

Kevin answered the phone on the second ring yelling, "What the fuck is your problem?"

"Kevin what are you talking about?" India asked trying to act like she didn't know what he was talking about.

"India don't play dumb. I have been calling your simple ass all night. I don't want to hear that "I forgot my phone" either." Kevin said angrily.

"I really did forget my phone." India said not really paying Kevin any attention.

"Well why you didn't call me when you got in the house?" Kevin asked.

"Because I went right to sleep. I didn't even look at my phone." India said.

"Yeah, whatever. I got to go. Bye." Kevin said hanging up on her.

India just looked at the phone as to say "*I know this mother fucker didn't hang up on me*". India didn't care about Kevin's attitude. She called her parents' house to check on her children. After getting off the phone with her parents, she made her something to eat, looked over her cases, and then ran her some bath water. She got in the bath tub and began to relax until her phone rung.

"Hello?" India said.

"What's up boo?"

"Ain't shit Kim, just taking a bath." India said.

"It's about time you taking a bath with your dirty ass." Kim joked.

"I see you have jokes." India said still laughing at Kim.

"Any who, I am not going to be able to go out tonight."

Before Kim could explain India said "You suck! Why? What Quan won't allow you to go out?"

Kim laughed real hard at her friend then said "The reason I can't go is because my baby is sick. He has a fever and stomachache. Plus Quan don't run anything I do."

"Oh ok. Take care of my baby, and yea right where is Quan at anyway?" India said.

"Right here sick as well. So you know that's two babies I have to take care of." Kim said

"Good luck with that."

India and Kim talked a little more than they got off the phone with each other, promising to talk the next day.

India put on a short dress and waited for her cousin Peaches to come and pick her up. India got into the car she noticed that all of Peaches friends she brought with her were hoes. She wished someone would have come with her.

"Yo, which club we going to?" India asked.

"We going to club "Nightmare"." Lyric, who was one of Peaches friends, answered.

Club nightmare was known to live up to its name. It was located in the worst part of DC and it was never a night when the club is not on the news. It was always a fight, shoot out or something.

"Why are we going to this ghetto club?" India asked.

"Girl, this is the spot on Saturdays." Lyric said twerking in her seat.

India just shook her head and texted Kim where they were just in case something popped off.

When they got in the club they saw that it was popping. Not even 15 minutes into their fun, a fight broke out, but that ain't stop them from partying. India saw some of the dudes she use to fuck, and some she even dissed, but they ain't stop her from having fun either.

"Yo, India." A random guy called out her name.

India turned around and noticed it was one of the dudes she used to mess with.

"Hey Melvin." India said dryly.

Even though Melvin was sexy, had money, and was good in bed, he was an asshole. He had a rep of whipping his women but India never witnessed that side of him.

"Damn baby, you look good. Where you been hiding?" Melvin asked eyeing India up and down.

"I've been around." India said sipping her drink.

"So when can a brother get up in that tight pussy?" Melvin asked.

"You won't. I have a man." India said.

"Well, he ain't doing a good job because you over here flirting with me." Melvin said licking his lips.

"Look bye Melvin. Get out of my face." India said, while turning away from him.

India got up from the bar and was headed towards Peaches and her friends, when Melvin grabbed her arm.

"Don't walk away from me bitch." Melvin said angrily.

"Get off of me." India said trying to pull her arm from his grasp. Melvin seemed to pull on her arm tighter after that.

"Look, you going to give me some of this pussy or I'm going to take it." Melvin said while pulling India close to him. She was so close to him that she could feel how hard he was.

Melvin traced his fingers on India's upper thigh, inching up her dress. She was trying to get away but his grip was too tight.

"What the fuck is this?" A voice yelled. It was a voice that India knew so well and was more than happy to hear.

With tears in her eyes, she was so happy to see Kevin.

"Dawg, what the fuck you doing with my girl?" Kevin asked stepping to Melvin.

"Look you need to step. I'm trying to handle my business." Melvin said standing up. His hand was still holding India's arm, surely leaving a bruise from the grip.

Kevin was getting pissed "Babe lets go before I have to lay this nigga flat."

"He has my arm baby. I have been trying to get loose for a long time." India said still trying to get away.

Kevin turned to Melvin and punched him square in his jaw. Before anyone could blink, Melvin fell to the floor unconscious. India immediately stepped away from him and went towards Kevin.

"What I tell you?" Kevin said while he grabbed India's hand, leading her out the club.

"You weren't supposed to be back till tomorrow. How you know where I was at anyway?" India asked following Kevin.

"I have eyes everywhere. Come on let's get out of here. I hate the sight of this club." Kevin said.

Kevin and India were walking to the car where Shawn had it parked out front of the club. When they exited, they noticed that some dudes were behind them.

"Go get in the car ma." Kevin said.

India got in the car without a fight while Shawn got out.

"So you just going to take my man's girl and step." One of the guys said.

"I ain't for no talking, it is what it is." Kevin said.

"Man fuck you, you bitch." Another dude said.

Kevin was tired of the talk coming from the dudes and was trying to get home, so he pulled out his gun.

"What's it going to be?" Kevin asked cocking the gun.

The dudes realized that they weren't strapped and knew Kevin wasn't playing. Deciding it wasn't a fight they wanted parts of; they turned around and went back into the club.

"What up sis." Shawn said when he got in the car.

"Hey Shawn. How y'all know where I was?" India asked Shawn because she knew he would tell her.

"Who you think?" Shawn said.

"Kim?" India asked.

"Dawg, I told you Kim knew where she was; now you owe me $200." Kevin said getting into the front seat.

India rode quietly in the back, sending Peaches a text that she left the club with Kevin.

Chapter 28

London

"Girl, this nigga messes up all types of surprises." London said on the phone while talking to Lisa.

"What he do now?" Lisa asked.

"Ever since that incident between me and Keith, I can't separate from BJ." London said.

"You know he just trying to protect you. So what you have planned for tonight?" Lisa asked.

"Tonight Landon is going to watch Bryant and I planned dinner and you know what's next." London said.

"That's what's up."

"The only thing is that I have to go pick up some stuff but BJ want to follow me everywhere." London said.

"Girl just sneak out." Lisa told her.

"I just might have to do that. Speaking of Mr. nosey here he comes, I'll call you back." London said and got off the phone with Lisa. Hiding the things she was going to use for tonight, London walked out her bedroom right into BJ.

"Where you about to go?" BJ asked.

"I'm about to go to the store. You need something?" London asked.

"You ain't going by yourself."

"I'll be alright." London said waving him off.

"Yeah whatever ma. I'm going down stairs. Let me know when you are ready." BJ said, walking away.

London thought about what Lisa told her to do and got her car keys and purse and headed out the side door downstairs. When London pulled out the drive way her cell phone rang.

"Yes Brandon." London said after looking at the screen.

"So you know that was wrong." BJ said

"What I do that was wrong?" London said, faking innocence.

"You know I don't want you out by yourself till I get that lil punk ass bitch."

"I know babe, but I'll be fine, trust me. I just have to handle some business and I'll be right back in the house." London said.

"Iight I'll be waiting." BJ said.

London hung up the phone and got everything that she needed to make the evening perfect. When she got everything that she needed she headed back home. Pulling up, she noticed that BJ's car wasn't outside so she took everything in the house and started to prepare for the evening. She started cooking BJ favorite meal which was lamb chops, yellow rice and steamed veggies. She also made his favorite desert: strawberry cheese cake. By the time dinner was done, BJ was walking through the door.

"Damn, it smells good in here." BJ said.

"Come in the dining room." London said when she heard BJ voice.

When he walked in the dining room he was shocked of what London had on. She stood in front of him with red pumps and a black negligee on.

"Damn ma, you look good." BJ said walking towards her and giving her a kiss on the lips. He started to grab her around the waist and pull her towards the stairs.

"Stop silly and sit down before your food gets cold." London said trying to get out of BJ's embrace.

"The only thing I want to eat is you." BJ said still holding her close.

London was able to get out of BJ's arms. Even though he pouted at her, he sat down at the table and watched as she brought over his plate of food. London put an extra swing to her hips, causing BJ's dick to twitch.

BJ and London ate their dinner and enjoyed each other's company.

"Yo, babe that was good as hell. What's next? You?"

"Nope. I have cheese cake. Then maybe me after that." London said sultrily.

London cut BJ a slice of cheesecake and handed it to him. While he ate the cheese cake she went upstairs to make sure everything was in order. When she got back down stairs BJ was done.

"That was fast babe. Are you ready for the next event?" London asked.

"Yeah I'm ready." BJ said licking his lips.

London grabbed BJ's hand and led him up the stairs. The room had rose petals on the bed with candles lit and massaging oil on the night stand.

"So, what's your plan with all of these oils and these candles? Looks like the makings of a house fire."

"Shut up and strip." London said.

BJ took his clothes off slow, and made sure that London never took her eyes of him. She looked at his perfect abs and watched as he stood before her naked, his dick aiming straight towards her. Every time she sees BJ naked, she always looks at him as if it is her first time seeing him.

"Now lay on the bed."

BJ laid on his stomach with his arms crossed in front of them. London grabbed the warming oil from the dresser and placed some in her hands, rubbing them together to test he temperature. She began to massage him slowly, starting with his upper back and moving lower.

"Damn that feels good." BJ said loving London's hands on him.

"Oh really. Lay on your back." London said.

BJ did as he was told. London massaged his chest, legs, and then his member. She massaged it till it was rock hard. Bending down over BJ, she replaced her hands with her mouth.

"Oh shit…" BJ said as London showed her skill.

She kept on sucking till BJ's toes curled up and he had a stuck face. She stopped so BJ could calm down. She didn't want him to cum just yet.

"You good baby?" London asked.

"Hell Yeah! Why you stop?" BJ asked with a smile on his face.

"Because, you were not going to cum in my mouth." London said.

"You know I wouldn't do that. So can I cum in you then?" BJ asked.

"No." London said sternly.

"Ma, I been meaning to ask you. Why lately when we have sex you always have me use condoms? We ain't ever use to them before." BJ asked sitting up.

"I have my own personal reasons." London said, not meeting his eyes.

"Which are?"

"Look I don't want to talk about it. Can we just continue the night?"

"Naw, because I want to know what's the deal with you."

"Look, I don't want to get pregnant again. I'm not ready for anymore children."

"Why you just ain't tell me that. I can respect that. I love you. We'll have more children when you are ready. Now let's finish this night out. But just so you know, I'm not using a condom tonight. I'll pull out, but I wanna feel you with no latex."

"I love you too, and you don't have to as long as you pull out."

London and BJ made love all night long. When they were done they took a shower together and fell asleep in each other's arms.

Chapter 29

Lorren

"I can't believe I'm about to go out with Mat. Rico is going to kill me if he finds out. Rico might kill me but this is the only way I can make sure there is nothing between me and Mat." Lorren took her children to her mother's house so Landon could babysit. She told Rico she was chilling with the girls so she could get away.

Lorren pulled up at the theater late because she knew Mat was never on time. When she parked she noticed that Mat was in the front of the theater waiting.

"Oh you on time today." Lorren said when she walked up to him.

"See Miss Lorren a lot of things have changed." Mat said casually with his hands in his pockets.

"What else has changed?" Lorren said in a flirtatious way.

"You would have to see that later." Mat said pulling her close to him for a hug.

Lorren couldn't help but love the feeling of being in his arms, but she knew she had to break away because she liked the feeling way too much.

"So what are we going to see?" Lorren asked breaking away from Mat.

"It's your choice sweetheart." Mat said.

Lorren picked a movie which was not scary so she wouldn't be all on Mat and she didn't pick a romantic flick because she didn't want to send him the wrong message. So she picked a comedy movie. They enjoyed the movie and after the movie he took her to dinner. Pulling up to Kobe Japanese Steakhouse, they were seated immediately next to a young couple.

"You remember when we were that age?" Mat asked Lorren.

"Yeah, when we were that age, we were doing things we had no business doing." Lorren said.

They both got quiet thinking about their teen years. Their train of thought was interrupted by the waitress.

"May I take your drink order?" the waitress asked.

"I'll have a Buddha" Lorren said.

"I'll have a beer." Mat said.

When the waitress left with their drink order along with their food order, they began to talk.

"So how you been Lorren?"

"I been well, I can't complain." Lorren said.

"So how long have you been talking to your boyfriend?" Mat asked, getting right to the point.

"We have been together for about 9 years." Lorren said.

"So you started talking to him right after me?" Mat said, raising an eyebrow at that.

170

"When you got locked up, he was already my friend. I knew him for a long time. He would come pass my job when I would come home on breaks from school. When you got locked up, I just started talking to him seriously."

"Oh true. So how many kids you have?"

"I have two. Rico is 7 and Lacey is 2."

"So how does he treat you? Because word around the way is that they want to put your nigga in a body bag."

"He treats me good. He's just real jealous."

Mat continued to quiz Lorren about her relationship with Rico. Every time he asked a question, Lorren would take a sip of her drink. After a while, her sipping caught up to her.

"You ready to go sexy?" Mat asked Lorren after he paid for the meal.

"Yeah, I'm so glad I dropped my car off at your house, because those drinks just sneaked up on me." Lorren said feeling more than tipsy.

"You were drinking it like it was Kool-Aid." Mat said laughing.

"I know right. So what's next? Are you going to show me what else has changed?" Lorren asked with lust in her eyes.

"If that's what you want Ms. Smith." Mat said.

"I do." Lorren said.

That was all Mat needed to hear. He grabbed Lorren's hand and they got in his car, headed to his place. They got out the car and they couldn't keep their hands off of each other as they entered his house. Mat picked Lorren up, never breaking their kiss. He placed her on the couch gently and then he began to kiss her neck, replacing his kisses with small bites. He moved from her neck down her V-neck shirt. He was making Lorren feel so light headed. He had his mouth on her breast, while his hand was in her pants. Pushing up slightly, Mat removed Lorren's jeans and underwear, throwing them off to the side. In one movement he replaced his mouth with his hand and his hand with his mouth. Lorren was feeling so good, but the better it felt the guiltier she became.

"Stop." Lorren said.

"What?" Mat said as he came up from between her legs.

"I can't do this. I have to go." Lorren was already grabbing her underwear and jeans from off the floor.

"Lorren you must be kidding." Mat said looking down at her like she was crazy.

"Look, I thought I still had feeling for you but I don't. I have to go Mat. I'm sorry; I'm in love with Rico."

"Iight do you." Mat said upset.

While Lorren was fixing her clothes her phone rung.

"Hello?" Lorren said already knowing who it was.

"Where you at baby?" Rico asked.

"I'm on my way home now." Lorren said with a feeling of guilt weighing on her chest.

"Alright come on, you know I can't sleep without you."

172

Lorren hung up the phone and ran out of Mat's house. She jumped in her car and raced home, never once looking back.

Chapter 30

Kim

"Quan lets go. We are going to be late." Kim yelled.

They were going to church with Kim's mother because Angel, Kim's sister, was dancing. Kim went to this church her whole life, but stopped going when she became a senior in high school. Before she had started dating Shawn she was dating this dude named Jacob. He was two years older than Kim and he ended up getting married on Kim. After that happened she stopped going to church.

"Iight ma here I come. You lucky I love your family because I still would have been sleep." Quan said.

"I'm going to make sure I tell ma that too." Kim said.

"You a little snitch. See even Xavier thinks it's too early. " Quan said picking Xavier up from off the couch.

They rode to church and when they pulled up, Kim had so many memories. When they got in the church it was youth Sunday, so all the kids were singing in the choir stand. They ushered them to sit by Mia Kim's mother.

"Grandma." Xavier said when they sat down.

"Hey baby. I'm glad y'all could make it." Mia said to Quan and Kim.

They enjoyed the service and listened intently to the word being spoken. Once church was over, all of the church folk told Kim they haven't seen her in awhile and talked a hole in her head.

"Babe, I can't take these fake church people anymore." Kim said to Quan.

"You ready to go?" Quan asked. He could tell the phony ones that were talking to Kim.

"Yeah, my feet hurt so can you go get the car." Kim asked.

Quan went to get the car while Kim talked to her aunt. While she was talking, she heard somebody call her name.

She turned around and was face to face with Jacob.

"Hey Kim."

"What's up Jacob?"

"Nothing. You are looking good."

"Thank you."

"So you came to see Angel dance?"

"Yeah and my mom asked me to come. Aren't you supposed to be catching up with your wife?" Kim asked trying to get Jacob out of her face.

"Oh we aren't together anymore."

Before Jacob could continue to talk Xavier and Angel came over.

"Kim, your son is so bad." Angel said.

"What he do?" Kim asked

175

"Ma no I didn't, grandma gave me the candy." Xavier said.

"I was just playing Kim. I told him if he doesn't tell me who gave him the candy, I was going to tell you he took it from somebody."

"Oh ok." Before Kim could say something else to Jacob, Quan pulled up.

Quan walked over and kissed Kim, then looked at Jacob and said "What's up player, you ready to go baby girl?"

"Yeah I'm ready." Kim got in the car not giving Jacob a second glance. As soon as Quan got in the car he started to quiz Kim.

"Who was that joker?" Quan asked as he drove to Kim's great grandmother's house for dinner.

"He was just somebody I dated when I was in high school." Kim said not in the mood.

"So what were y'all talking about?"

"Damn you nosey."

"See your ass always playing."

When they pulled up in front of her grandmother's house she saw a car she knew so well.

"What the fuck is he doing here?" Kim said.

She got out the car and walked in the house, Shawn was in the living room talking to her family.

"What's up y'all?" Shawn said to Kim, Quan and Xavier.

"Let me talk to you outside." Kim said pointing at Shawn.

Kim felt like everybody was testing her today.

"What's up cry baby?"

"Why are you here?"

"Your cousin invited me. So what? I'm not invited around the family anymore?"

"No you not. So I think you should leave."

"Yo, you straight tripping." Shawn said.

"Fine, have it your way." Kim went back in the house and spoke to her family. She told them she was leaving to avoid any conflict.

"Quan lets go." Kim said.

"We just got here and I'm hungry." Quan said looking at Kim with disbelief.

"Look Quan let's go. I'm not feeling it here." Kim said.

Quan didn't feel like getting into it with Kim so they left. They went out to eat at Red Lobster instead. When they made it home, Kim went and read, while Quan played the game with Xavier.

"It time for you to take a bath little man." Kim said to Xavier.

She gave him a bath and as soon as he got out he was out like a light. She went into the room and Quan was lying across the bed.

"Hey miss mean ass." Quan said.

"I'm not mean." Kim responded, rolling her eyes.

"You were straight tripping today."

"You just don't understand. He just keeps showing up." Kim said getting undressed.

"Well, stop letting him control your attitude." Quan said while looking at Kim get undressed.

"Yeah I know. What are you looking at?" Kim asked.

"I'm looking at that phat ass of yours. Yo, do that little dance you use to do." Quan said.

Quan turned on the radio, and Kim gave her man a lap dance that he always seemed to love. He calls her his private stripper. While dancing, she took off her remaining clothes. Getting naked she decided to undress Quan. She went to her knee and started to suck his dick just the way he liked it. His eyes closed and toes curled up immediately. Kim wanted to control the show, so she got on top of him, placing him inside her, and started to ride.

Her cell phone started to ring back to back while she was in the moment. She just continued to do what she was doing, not paying attention to anything but Quan. When she and Quan reached their climax they both fell out on the bed.

Kim picked up here phone and realized that Shawn was the person calling her phone. She grabbed her robe and went to the bathroom to take a shower. She turned on the shower water and called Shawn.

"Hello?" Shawn said when he picked up the phone.

"What's up? You kept calling me. Why?" Kim said.

"I want to let you know I love you and I hate when you don't want to be around me."

"Please don't do this to me Shawn; I can't take this right now."

"I know but I have to let you know how I feel." Shawn said.

Kim was about to say something when she heard Quan "Kim you iight in there?"

"Yeah, I'm good." Kim said to Quan.

"I have to go Shawn." Kim said. As soon as she hung up the phone, the bathroom door opened.

"Who were you on the phone with?" Quan asked.

"That was Danni." Kim said.

"Oh true." Quan said.

"Come on and take a shower with me." Kim said. When they got in the shower together, the only thing on Kim's mind was, *"Shawn is gonna get me killed."*

179

Chapter 31

Danni

"Moe, I feel like something is going to happen today." Danni said. She was feeling weird ever since she woke up.

"What you mean?" Moe asked.

"I don't know. Are you going to Tracey's going away party?" Danni asked changing the subject.

"Yeah, but I'm going to leave early though." Moe said.

"So, do I get some before I go to work today?" Danni asked, smiling and rubbing up against him.

Moe didn't waste any time. He took the towel from around Danni and picked her up. Pulling his boxers down, he led his self-inside of her. While holding her, he showed his strength by standing up and working Danni at the same time. While he held her, Danni arched her back so Moe could go deeper. She loved every moment of Moe loving. He put Danni down and bent her over the dresser and hit her from the back. He was giving it to Danni so good, she was calling his name in pleasure. When they exploded together, Danni went to take another shower so she could go to work.

When she arrived at work she was so relaxed and just wanted to get the day over with. She and Jaden joked around as they did every day. Jaden looked up when he spotted Danni's "patient".

"Hey Toni, you back for your follow up?" Danni asked.

"Yeah, I'm here for a follow up." Toni said.

180

Danni walked with Toni back to her examination room. Once she began to examine Toni, the questions started to roll again.

"When was the last time you saw my cousin?" Toni asked.

"The day I was hospitalized." Danni said, not in the mood for the questions.

"So why were you in the hospital?" Toni asked because she didn't know that part.

"Bryon beat me so I had to go to the hospital. What's with all the questions by the way?" Danni asked skeptically.

"I'm going to be truthful; I think you had my cousin killed." Toni said looking Danni in the eyes.

"What gives you that idea?" Danni asked showing no fear.

"You the only person who have a motive for having him murdered. Everybody loved my cousin."

"Well, I like your ideology but you looking and doing research on the wrong person." Danni said, washing her hands.

"I'm going to tell you one time and one time only. If you had something to do with my cousin death, you will have to deal with me." Toni said.

"Well, I'm going to tell you one time only, leave me alone before you have to deal with me. I also think it's best you find another OB/GYN to see as I am no longer willing to see you. Good day!" Danni said not backing down from Toni. With that said she left out the room and went to the break room to get her mind together. She was so happy Toni was her last patient for the day. She needed a breather. When she left work, she went to pick Genesis up and went home to change her clothes for the little dinner Tracey was having.-

Danni put on a skirt and a nice shirt with some cute sandals since it was a warm spring day. When she finished getting dressed, she called Moe to see where he was.

"Moe, I'm about to leave the house. I'll see you at Tracey's." Danni said.

"Ok, I'll be there shortly." Moe said.

Danni and Genesis got in the car and headed to Tracey's house. When she got there, all her friends were there. They all were there to celebrate Tracey's move. The only person who wasn't there was Zoe.

"Yo babe, I'm about to be out. I'll meet you at home." Moe said.

"Ok, I'm leaving in a few too." Danni said giving Moe a kiss.

"Why you leaving so early Danni?" Staci asked.

"Because I'm tired and my son has school tomorrow." Danni said.

"Damn bitch you could stay a little longer." Tracey said.

"Bitch you act like you leaving tomorrow. You ain't leaving for another two months." Danni said.

All the girls started to laugh when Danni said that. Danni said her good byes to everyone, and then she and Genesis left.

"You had fun with your cousins?" Danni asked her son looking into the rear view mirror at Genesis.

"Yes, I had fun."

While she talked to her son, she noticed a black impala had been trailing them for some time. She changed lanes but the car would change lanes with her. Danni began to get nervous but didn't want to alarm her son. All of a sudden sirens went off behind her, forcing her to pull over on the side of a deserted road.

The police officer walked to the car and Danni already had her license and registration out. When she rolled down the window, she noticed that it was the same cop who harassed her at her job.

"Hello Miss. Moore." Officer Jones said.

"May I ask why you are pulling me over officer?" Danni asked looking back at her son in the rearview mirror.

"I am going to need you to step out the car."

"What for? I haven't done anything. I have my son in the car." Danni said.

"I'm not going to say it again. Get out the car ma'am." Officer Jones said.

"Stay in the car honey and don't move ok" Danni said to her son.

"Ok mommy." Genesis said.

Danni got out the car and Officer Jones made her face the car and put her hands up on the hood. He faked like he was frisking her, but he was touching her inappropriately.

"So who murdered Bryon?" Officer Jones asked, putting his hand up her skirt.

"I don't know." Danni said holding back tears.

"So you are just going to lie to me. Would you lie to me if I fuck you on the front of your hood so your son can see?" Officer Jones asked stilling foundling her.

"Please, I don't know who killed him please let me go." Danni said crying now, no longer able to hold back the tears.

When Officer Jones was about to take it further he got a call on his radio.

"Shit. What they want now." Officer Jones said. Then he took the call.

Danni prayed that he would just leave.

"You lucky you bitch. I have to go. I'm going to get to the bottom of this case." Officer Jones said then got in his car.

Danni got in the car, hugging the steering wheel, and cried.

"Why are you crying mommy?"

"I love you." Danni said as she reached back to hug her son. She pulled off the side of the road in a trance. What would have happened if the Officer never got that call? Would he have made good on his threat? Those questions were circling in Danni's mind as she drove home. When Danni finally got in the house, she sat on the couch and held Genesis to her. Just thinking about what happened made her cry harder. Moe walked in the house to see his crying girlfriend holding his son.

"What happened? What's wrong?" Moe asked.

"He has to go." Danni said.

"Who has to go?"

"The officer."

"What happened?" Moe asked showing his anger.

"He touched me and told me he was going to rape me in front of Genesis." Danni said.

"What? I'm going to kill that nigga." Moe said getting angry.

"I know where you can find him." Danni said looking straight ahead.

"Where?" Moe asked with murder in his eyes.

"Toni." Danni said.

Part V

Pain hidden behind the smile!!!!

Chapter 32

Lisa

"Lisa Davis speaking." Lisa said into her office phone.

"Hello Ms. Davis. I was calling on behalf of Terence Davis." TJ's school called and said.

"Yes, what is the problem?" Lisa asked nervous.

"Well, today he and another student were fighting and he has a busted lip." The teacher said.

"Ok, I'm on my way." Lisa hopped up from her desk so quick and ran out the office to check on her son.

While she was in the car, she called Terence and there was no answer, she continued to call over and over again to get no answer from him. When she arrived at the school, she went to the principal's office where TJ was sitting there with an ice pack on his lip.

"What happened TJ?"

"We was playing basketball and I made a lot of shots and he got mad and hit me." TJ said.

Lisa didn't like anybody playing with her child. She was ready to fight the other child's mother for her son's busted lip. Lisa got real ghetto in the school office. She didn't care if the children were only in pre K, she was letting them all have it.

After she cursed the administrators out, she got in her car and headed back to work with her son.

"TJ is your lip fine?" Lisa asked.

"Yes mommy. I'm hungry."

"What you want to eat?"

"McDonalds."

Lisa looked at her son and took him to McDonalds. They had a good evening together. Lisa went back to work, and while she worked, TJ colored on the floor and kept his self-busy.

"Lisa Davis" she said when her phone rung.

187

"What's up ma? You have been calling me?" Terence said.

"I have been calling because your son is sitting here with a busted lip. If you would answer your phone you would have known."

"My bad ma, I was handling some business. What is wrong with you anyway? Is it that time of the month?" Terence asked not sure what was wrong with Lisa.

"My problem is that you care about that damn business or whatever it is more than me and your son. I don't feel like talking. Good bye." Lisa hung up the phone. She was ready to leave work after talking to Terence because she couldn't focus. He just knew how to get under her skin. All she wanted him to do was answer the phone when she called.

When she got home, she checked the mail while TJ went to play video games. She saw the letter that had "*CONFIDENTIAL*" on it addressed to Terence. Lisa's heart was beating fast. She opened the envelope and tears started to stream down her face.

"Why you crying sexy?" Terence asked when he walked in the house.

Lisa didn't say anything. She just passed him the letter.

"Why you crying, this proves I'm not the father." Terence said.

"I know Terence, but I don't know how much more of this I can take."

188

"Look, I'm confused. You have to break this down to me."

"I would have never thought I would have fallen in love with a drug dealer. Now that I have, it's hard for me to continue this life with you. I have to wonder "did my man sleep with you?", or is another girl going to call me telling me that her baby is yours."

"So what are you trying to say?" Terence asked getting pissed off.

"I don't know if the police are going to bust through here and take you or worse if somebody takes you from me." Lisa was crying while she talked.

"Lisa what the fuck you trying to say?" Terence asked again.

"I can't do this anymore. I love you so much, but I can't marry you or be with you anymore. TJ and I are going to move back in my grandmother's house." Lisa said.

"What? You have to be fucking kidding me. Yo Lisa I'm not going to let you go. You are the best thing that ever happened to me. You can't leave me baby." Terence said crying.

Before Terence had come home, Lisa had already packed most of her and TJ's clothes.

"I'm sorry baby. I love you so much but I need to do this." Lisa said giving Terence a kiss on the lips.

TJ came downstairs seeing both of his parents crying.

"Daddy why are you crying?" TJ asked.

Terence picked him up and held him so tight. Still crying he held his son close to his chest.

"I love you. Take care of your mom. You understand me?" Terence said looking his son in the eyes.

"I love you too, I understand. I'm a big boy." TJ said smiling at his dad.

Terence smiled back and said "iight big boy."

"Come on TJ" Lisa said.

She put their clothes in the car. Then she looked at Terence again and said "I love you."

"I love you too." Terence said, and they kissed for the last time.

Terence stood in the drive way looking at his son and wife back out the drive way and out of his life.

Chapter 33

Tracey

Tracey couldn't hide the tears as her students and staff threw her a going away party. She could admit she was going to miss every last one of them. Tracey was leaving next Friday, but she was using that time to get everything under situated.

"I am really going to miss all of you." Tracey told the staff and students.

Tracey packed up all of her belongings and took them to her car. Zoe was going to pick up Handsome so she didn't have to rush home. She was going to happy hour with Staci and Fran, one of her childhood friends.

"Girls, thank y'all for going out with me. Everybody else was busy." Tracey said.

"No problem, I know how it is." Staci said.

They were drinking and having a good time talking. Out the corner or Tracey's eye, she could see Kenny walking over to them.

"What's up beautiful?" Kenny said smiling.

"Are you following me or something?" Tracey asked.

"No, you just seem to be everywhere I am." Kenny said.

"Oh you a punk ass nigga you know that. How you going shoot at me and my fam?" Tracey asked not forgetting about the shooting after Kevin's party.

"What you talking about? After me and your boyfriend fought I went home." Kenny said.

"So you didn't shoot at us?"

"Come on Tracey, you know that's not my style. Plus why would I shoot anywhere near you?" Kenny said.

"I know that wasn't your MO. So how you been?"

"I have been ok. I miss you and want you back in my life." Kenny said seriously.

"That's sweet but I'm leaving Friday and you know I have a boyfriend."

"He doesn't treat you like I would. Where ever you go, I would come if you want me to." Kenny said.

Tracey was feeling the pressure of Zoe keep turning her down, and getting the attention from Kenny made her not think straight.

"Come with me." Tracey said pulling Kenny by the hand.

She led Kenny to the ladies bathroom. They went into a stall. When they got in, they were kissing, rubbing and touching.

The drinks had Tracey not thinking about what she was doing. Kenny sat on the toilet seat with his pants around his ankles while Tracey hiked her skirt up, pulling her panties to the side. Kenny made Tracey squat over him while he entered her. She was feeling good and so was Kenny. They were so in their zone that Tracey didn't hear her phone ring. When they climaxed, Tracey jumped up.

192

"Kenny this was fun and all but this is the last time we will ever see each other." Tracey said.

"What you mean? So I was just a quickie?" Kenny asked not liking the fact of being used.

"Call it what you want." Tracey said shrugging.

"How would you feel if I go and tell your boyfriend that I just fucked his girl in the bathroom?"

"To be honest that wouldn't be good on your behalf because he would kill you." Tracey said.

"Yeah we'll just see about that you hoe." Kenny said angrily.

Tracey fixed her clothes and walked out of the bathroom leaving Kenny there talking smack.

"Y'all I'm about to go home." Tracey said. They all hugged and Tracey left. When she got in the car she felt so nasty. All she wanted to do was go in the house and take a shower.

"Hey mommy." Tracey heard when she got in house.

"Hey baby. Where is your dad?" Tracey asked her son.

"He in the back." Handsome said.

"Ok, did you eat?"

"Yes, I had chicken."

"Ok, I'm about to go take a shower." Tracey told her son then headed to the bathroom upstairs.

Tracey was in the shower when the bathroom door opened.

"So, you got this letter with your so called new address on it." Zoe said.

"Zoe, I'm not in the mood for this right now." Tracey said trying to relax in the shower.

"I already told you that you not going so you need to chill." Zoe said.

Tracey cut the shower water off and wrapped her towel around her, looking at Zoe and walked out of the bedroom.

"Don't walk away from me." Zoe said.

"Look I know what it is. You are scared of change, but I'm going to tell you like this. It's going to be a change whether you like it or not, cause I'm going to California if you are on that plane next to me or not. This is my life and I am going to live it." Tracey said.

"I love you and I want you to have the best life ever but you are not going." Zoe said.

"We will see on Friday." Tracey said.

Zoe couldn't stand the fact that she might really leave him, so he walked out the room and left the house.

Chapter 34

London

"Yo, London why you been walking around all sad and shit?" India asked

"Shut up ain't nobody been walking around depressed, but Tracey and Lisa." London said.

"You have been looking kind of sad." Kim said.

All of the girls were at London house for dinner. London has been feeling down and depressed but she didn't know where it came from. She had everything in her life she could ever ask for.

"So sis you not going to tell us what's wrong." Lorren asked.

"Well it's like this. I have been feeling depressed but I have no reason to because nothing's been wrong. I have been feeling sick, and everything." London said.

"Did you take a pregnancy test?" Tracey asked eyeing her.

"No, because I know I'm not pregnant." London said sternly.

"How do you know that?" Lisa asked.

"I make sure that BJ wrap up all the time." London said.

"That still doesn't mean anything London." Danni said. If anything, she knew condoms could break easily.

"Well, I'll take the test so y'all can shut up. We have to go to the store and get one." London said.

"No we don't, I have one right here." Kim said going through her purse.

"Why in the hell do you have a pregnancy test in your purse?" India asked.

"I have too many scares, so to keep me from wondering I just keep one in my purse." Kim said.

London grabbed the test from Kim and went to the bathroom. She eyed the test on the counter for a couple of minutes before deciding to open it. After doing her business and peeing on the stick, she placed it on the counter and waited for the results. After 3 minutes, she started to see a second line form next to the first. Grasping the stick in her hand, she knew that she was pregnant. Walking out the bathroom on autopilot, she sat on the couch next to Lorren.

"So what does it say?" Lisa asked.

London passed the test to Danni. She couldn't even form a sentence she was so mad. She could have sworn that she and BJ were careful with using protection or him pulling out.

"So you're pregnant. That's nothing to be mad about London." Danni said.

"Do y'all remember when I told y'all I don't think I can do anymore children?" London asked still staring straight ahead. All the girls nodded in agreement. "Well, I think I'm going to get an abortion. I can't do the pregnancy thing." London said bursting out crying.

"London, that is so damn selfish. At least see what BJ want to do." Lorren said.

"It's my damn body that will have to go through this. He should understand." London said angrily.

The girls sat there and talked a little more until BJ walked into the house.

"Hey ladies." BJ said when he walked into the house.

"Hey brother." All the ladies said in unison. BJ smiled at that.

"We about to go." India said to London and BJ.

When the girls left, London found BJ upstairs watching TV.

"So, what you and your girls were talking about?" BJ asked flipping to ESPN to catch some game highlights.

"You know just regular stuff. What you been up too?" London asked.

"I've just been on the hunt. You know. Nothing out the usual." BJ said.

"Well, baby I have something important to talk to you about." London said.

"OK, I'm all ears." BJ said turning the TV off and looking at her.

"Well, do you remember when I told you about my issues? Well…" Before London could finish BJ's phone rung and he asked her to hold for a minute.

"What? Give me good news only." BJ said into the phone. "Bet son, I'm on my way." He hung up the phone, went in the closet and came back out. "Babe, we'll continue this when I get back. Love you." BJ said kissing London on the lips as he left the house.

London sat in the house thinking about the pros and cons about having the baby. She called someone who she knew would always have her back: her mother.

"Hey ma." London said when her mother answered the phone.

"Hey London. What's the matter honey?" Lacey asked.

"I just found out I am pregnant again." London said.

"That is good news honey. Why do you sound so sad though?"

"Well, after I had Bryant I went into depression and I don't think I can go through that again. Not to mention I'm moving up in my career. I think a child another child would slow me down." London said.

"Baby girl, you might go through depression the first time but you don't know if you'll go through it this time. A lot of women after having their baby suffer from depression. It's natural baby. What do Brandon have to say about it?"

"I haven't talked to him yet."

"Well, pray on it and think about what you plan on doing. You know I will gladly welcome another grandbaby. " Lacey said.

"Thanks ma. Love you."

"No problem baby, love you too."

London felt a little better when she got off the phone. Deciding to take her mom's advice, she prayed on the situation at hand. After praying, she felt tired and knew that a nap was needed. Since Bryant was over BJ's mother house, she was ok to sleep for a couple of hours.

While London was in a deep sleep she felt BJ sit on the bed. His back was to her but she could feel the tension coming off him in waves.

"What's wrong BJ?" London asked.

"Nothing." He said, taking off his clothes and going into the bathroom. London got up and followed him. When she looked at him she saw the blood coating him.

"Are you ok?" London asked worriedly.

"I'm fine. I had to handle some business." BJ said nonchalantly.

"What type of business?" London asked.

"Don't worry about it. Go back to bed." BJ said.

London just stood there and watched BJ get in the shower. With her clothes still on she got in with him.

"What are you doing, London?" BJ asked looking at her like she was crazy.

"I have to talk to you. It's very important and can't wait." London said.

BJ faced her and gave her his attention.

Blowing out a harsh breath, London said, "I'm pregnant."

BJ smiled and looked down at her. He started to kiss and hug her, showing his joy.

"I'm not keeping it though." London said avoiding eye contact.

"What?" BJ said with pain in his eyes.

"I'm sorry but, this is something I had to tell you. I'm going to see Danni tomorrow to see how far along I am then I'm going to get the abortion." London said grabbing the hem of her wet shirt.

Tears rolled down BJ eyes and London couldn't bear to look at him. She stepped out of the shower, knowing she cause his heartache. Once she got into their room, she broke down crying. Walking to her dresser, she put on some dry clothes. BJ didn't want to be near her or even breathe in her scent. He put on some clothes after his shower, grabbed his keys and left the house. London knew she was in the wrong, so she called him, but there was no answer. She continued to call him all night with the same results.

Chapter 35

Lorren

"Rico I don't trust my kids with your family." Lorren said after leaving Rico's family house. They just dropped the children off at Rico parent's house. Rico's mother never liked Lorren from when they first started dating, but the feelings were mutual with Lorren.

"Why you always have to start it with my family?" Rico asked.

"Since I'm black they always have something to say." Lorren said.

"My family loves you. They don't care that you black."

"Yeah whatever. If your mom calls me one more "heffa" I'm going to call immigration." Lorren said laughing.

"Yo, stop playing with my family. They have their green cards. Who is that that keep calling your phone?" Rico asked after hearing Lorren's phone for the 3rd time. Her phone had been vibrating off the hook, but she wouldn't answer it.

"It's nobody." Lorren said. As soon as Lorren said that her phone vibrated again.

"So you telling me that's nobody." Rico asked.

"Yeah, that's what I'm saying." Lorren said changing her phone to silent.

Rico grabbed Lorren's phone and saw all the missed calls. While he was looking through the missed calls, a text message popped up.

"I hate that you love that nigga so much when you know you supposed to be with me. The last time we were together was too perfect. Hit a nigga up when you come to your senses." Rico read the text message out loud.

"So what happened the last time you and Mat was together? Hold up, when were you and Mat together?" Rico asked.

"What?" Lorren asked playing dumb.

"You heard what I said. Don't make me hit reply and ask myself."

"We went to a movie and dinner about two or three months ago. That's it?"

"You lied to me. Why you go out with this nigga? Tell me everything before I get pissed off." Rico said clenching her phone.

"Look I told you we went to a dinner and movie." Lorren said praying that he didn't do anything stupid.

"Yeah we'll see what happened?" Rico said. Lorren noticed that Rico was driving the opposite way from their house.

"Where are we going?" Lorren asked anxiously.

"We going to find out what happened the night y'all were together." Rico said.

"I told you. What you don't believe me?" Lorren asked.

"I believe you, but it seems like you not telling me the whole truth. So let me know right fucking now Lorren. Cause we can make this visit."

"I lied to you when we first met. I told you I was a virgin, but I wasn't. I only did it about 2 times. Mat was my first. After I saw him at Kevin's party I couldn't get him off my mind, so to make sure there wasn't anything there I asked him out. We went out and I realized that you were the only one for me." Lorren said, telling Rico most of the facts.

"So it took you to go out with this nigga to make you realize that you want to be with me?"

"No, it's not like that Rico."

"Well, we about to see how much you love me or want to be with that nigga." Rico said.

Rico drove around the neighborhood where Mat hung at. Rico knew the neighborhood too well because Lorren and London use to hang around the same hood. He rode around slowly until he spotted his target. He saw Mat coming from out of the corner store.

"Yo, Mat. Let me holla at you?" Rico said pulling up alongside him.

"What's up player? Hey Lorren." Mat said smirking.

Rico got out the car. "You stay in the car." Rico said to Lorren while slamming the car door.

Lorren took a deep breath and shook her head.

"So Mat, you had sex with my wife?" Rico asked.

"Man that was way back in high school." Mat said.

"So, what happened the other night y'all were together?" Rico asked.

203

"Oh I see what this is. You scared that your girl might be feeling someone else. You want me to tell you what Lorren and I did so your ass can start some shit and then get all piss off at her."

"You don't know shit. Plus a scared pussy like you taking my woman that will never happen." Rico said getting in Mat's face.

"Yo, back the fuck up from my face man. So you really want to know what me and Lorren did? I ate that sweet pussy of hers. Oh was it good too. Just like I remembered. Wet and everything." Mat said with a smirk.

Before the smirk left Mat face, Rico had punched him. The two of them began to fight in the middle of the street, drawing a small crowd. Lorren jumped out the car, rushing to Rico.

"Rico, stop… Rico stop." Lorren yelled.

At this time Rico had pulled his gun out and had it in Mat's face.

"Rico, stop what are you doing?" Lorren asked trying to calm him down.

"So, are you taking up for this nigga now? So you want to be with this nigga? Huh? Is that it?" Rico asked breathing heavily.

"Baby you not thinking straight, put the gun up and let's go. I want to be with you. I love you, let's go home please." Lorren pleaded.

Rico got up but not putting his gun away and got in the car.

"I'm sorry Mat." Lorren said.

Mat looked at Lorren and before he could say something Rico said "Lorren bring your ass."

Lorren got in the car and didn't say anything the whole ride home.

"You make me do crazy shit like that Lorren. I love you so much but you make me want to kill somebody for looking at you. I hate that! I should have killed him." Rico said banging his fist on the steering wheel.

While Rico went on and on Lorren just looked at him, thinking ***"I hope he is not back to his old ways."***

Chapter 36

India

India cleaned up her house while talking with Kim on the phone.

"Girl, this nigga got me cleaning like I'm a fucking maid." India said exhausted.

"Why the hell are you cleaning and cooking slave child?" Kim said laughing.

"His damn cousin is coming to town." India said.

"Girl, Kevin is going to be showing off." Kim said.

"Yeah, I know he is. I'm just preparing myself for this shit. I miss my damn kids." India said.

"Where the hell are your kids? Every time I call they are gone somewhere." Kim asked.

"You know my parents love to travel. They are gone to Florida to visit family." India said.

"Shit they should have taken me." Kim said seriously.

"Bitch who you telling? If I was gone I won't be in this damn house cooking and cleaning like I'm waiting for massah to come home."

India and Kim were laughing and cracking jokes. Then she heard the door open and male voices.

"Girl, they are here and that damn baby father of yours is here too." India said. "I can hear his ass clear as day."

"Go get ready little slave girl… and please don't tell Shawn you are talking to me." Kim said.

"What's up baby? It smells good in here. Oh what's up Kim, I know your ass is on the phone." Kevin said walking up to India.

"Kim you heard that." India said into the phone.

"Bye, India, have fun serving." Kim laughed, hanging up.

"Come on and meet my cousin." Kevin said.

India walked into the living room where Shawn and Kevin's cousin was at.

"Yo, Calvin this is my wifey India. India this is my cousin Calvin." Kevin said.

"Hey, nice to meet you Calvin. What's up Shawn with your punk ass?" India said.

"Ain't shit sis. What is my wife doing?" Shawn asked.

"If you mean Kim, she is at home. Probably with her Man." India said walking out the living room.

"Yo, your wifey looks familiar cuz." Calvin said.

"Man, shut up you don't know India." Shawn said.

While the guys were in the living room talking, India was in the kitchen thinking hard because Calvin looked so familiar, but she couldn't remember where she knows him from.

"Y'all the food is ready." India yelled to the guys. All of them came to the table. They were eating like they had been starved before that point.

"So, India what do you do for a living?" Calvin asked.

"I'm a lawyer." India said.

"You look familiar. Did you ever come to New York before?" Calvin asked.

"Yeah you look familiar too. I went to New York when my girl London was doing an internship up there." India said, thinking back to how long ago that was.

"Did y'all go to a club?" Calvin asked.

"It was like 8 girls in New York. Yeah we went to a club." India said.

"Damn nigga you asking a lot of questions. Just face that you don't know her." Kevin said.

"Yeah, you right cuz." Calvin said.

They continued to eat. When everyone was done eating, Kevin looked at India and said "You got the dishes?"

India looked at Kevin and said "You pushing it. You going to do the dishes and Shawn ass is going to take out the trash. I'm not a house wife or a maid. I'm going to take a shower. You understand?"

Kevin just looked at India and smiled. He loved when India gave orders. "Yo, Shawn! India said your ass taking out the trash while I do the dishes." Kevin said.

"Dawg, I don't live here." Shawn complained.

"Well, stop eating here then." India yelled while walking upstairs.

All of the guys started to laugh.

"Welcome to the family son." Kevin said.

While the guys straightened up downstairs, India was really trying to think where she knew Calvin from. She called Kim back.

"Yo, bitch I got a problem." India said.

"What is it?" Kim asked.

"Kevin's cousin looks so familiar. I hope I didn't mess with him before." India said.

"You and me both. That would be fucked up. Does he remember you?" Kim asked.

"Yes girl, he was asking me all these questions and shit. Oh shit I do remember him. Don't you remember when we all went to New York to visit London and we went to the club and a group of niggas were flashing their money and shit. Then we took all their money and told them we would meet them at the hotel but never showed up." India said.

"Oh yeah, I do remember that. We told them all types of shit. They were giving us money like it was nothing. Then we sent the prostitutes to their rooms so we wouldn't have to go." Kim said laughing like shit.

"Hell yeah. We told the prostitutes to keep the light off at all times." India said laughing hard.

"Hell yeah. I wish I was there to see their faces." Kim said.

"Nigga one of the guys is Kevin cousin, son. This is going to be a long visit." India said.

While India was upstairs talking to Kim on the phone, the guys were downstairs smoking and talking.

"Yo, cuz, I know where I know India from now." Calvin said.

"Where?" Kevin asked.

"I hate to tell you this but I fucked her son." Calvin said.

"Man you a lie." Kevin said laughing it off.

"Naw, I'm for real. She was at the club with some bad ass chicks. Me and my boys fucked one of every friend that was there." Calvin said.

"So was a girl named Kim with her?" Shawn asked.

"Man, I don't know names. I know faces." Calvin said.

Kevin picked up a picture that India had with all of her friends and herself in it.

"So all of these girls were in a hotel room with one of your friends?" Kevin asked.

"Yep, every last one of them." Calvin said.

Kevin didn't say anything else. He got up and stormed upstairs. When he walked in the room he saw India on the phone laughing.

"Get the fuck off the phone. We need to talk." Kevin yelled.

The way he stepped to India shocked her. "Kim I'm going to call you back because this nigga is tripping." India said.

"You are such a hoe. I can't believe I'm in love with a hoe." Kevin said looking at India with disgust.

"Look Kevin, I'm not going to be too many more of your hoes. What the fuck is your problem?" India asked.

"You fucked my cousin?" Kevin asked.

"No I ain't fuck your cousin."

"Well, clearly he remembers fucking you. Who else have you fucked, so when they step to me I won't be shocked?" Kevin said.

"First, I don't fuck everybody I talk to. Second, that was my past and you knew that I had a long history of dudes when you first started talking to me. Third, I never fucked your cousin. Your cousin and his dumb ass friends were trying to play my girls and me like we were tricks, so we played them. You need to get your facts together before you ever step to me." India said pointing her finger at Kevin.

"Fuck you. I know you and your friends ain't shit but hoes. I don't know why I started talking to you. I should just knock your ass out." Kevin said stepping to India.

"Kevin please, I ain't want to be in a relationship in the first place. If you weren't so whipped by the pussy, I would still be living my life and not acting like a fake ass house wife. Fuck

211

you. As far as calling my girls hoes, nigga think again." India said.

"You want your life back… you want your fucking life back. Fine you can have it. I'll give you 3 weeks to find a fucking apartment, condo, or anything so you can live your fucking life. Till then I'm out and you be gone in 3 weeks." Kevin said brushing past her.

"Fuck you… I fucking hate you, you dumb ass bastard." India yelled as she heard the door slam.

Chapter 37

Danni

"What is going on with all of our friends' honey?" Danni asked Moe.

"I have no idea babe. As long as they don't bring that mess this way. We got enough stuff to deal with." Moe said.

"Yeah, I know. Speaking of our problem, I'm going to call and tell her I want to talk about her cousin and stuff, and most likely officer Jones will be close by." Danni said. She was tired of being threatened.

"That's good babe, take her to the house that we talked about, and the process will happen then." Moe said.

Danni and Moe had been working on a plan to get rid of their problems for a minute. Ever since India told her that she saw Toni at the police station, and Toni kept coming around, she started to think, "Maybe she is working with Officer Jones". Then it all came clear when she slipped up and said her boyfriend is with law enforcement. Danni didn't like being played for a fool so she was ready to do her deed.

"So are we doing this tonight?" Danni asked.

"Yeah, we have to while Staci is watching Genesis." Moe said.

"Yeah, I'm nervous baby." Danni said.

"Don't be. I'm here and I would never let anything happen to you." Moe said.

213

"I know. I just need this to go smoothly. I can't lose Genesis or you." Danni said.

"Trust me it is. Nothing is going to happen to my son or you. So let's get this started baby." Moe said.

Danni gave Moe a kiss as he left to go and make sure everything was in order for the plan tonight.

Danni took a deep breath and picked up her burner phone. When Toni had asked for her number, she gave her the cell that she used when people that she didn't normally talk asked for her number.

"Hello." Toni said.

"Hey, I need to talk to you, but I don't want to do it over the phone." Danni said.

"Ok, what is it that you want to talk about?" Toni asked.

"It's about your cousin. I'm going to come and pick you up so we can talk." Danni said.

Toni started to smile through the other end of the phone. She gave Danni the address and told her that she would be ready in 15 minutes. When Danni arrived to the house, Toni was ready.

"So where are your children?" Danni asked.

"Girl, they in the house. The oldest is babysitting." Toni said.

Danni just looked at her and shook her head.

"So where are we going?" Toni asked.

"Well, I'm thinking about buying another house. So since we have to talk, I figure that we could go see the place and have a conversation." Danni said.

"That's cool." Toni said.

Danni's phone rang while she was driving. Putting her earphones in, she answered.

"Hello?" Danni said.

"Hey baby you good?" Moe asked.

"Yeah, I'm good. I'm about to go see the place that I want to buy." Danni said.

"Ok right on time." Moe said.

Danni hung up the phone and looked at Toni. The quicker she got there, the quicker this could be over. Just having Toni in the same space as her was making her skin crawl.

"So, was that your boyfriend?" Toni asked.

"Yeah, it was." Danni said.

"So what is it that you want to talk about?" Toni asked.

"Well, I have a question first. Why are you so interested in me and your cousin's past relationship?" Danni asked turning on the street that had the house on it that she was looking for.

"I just want to know who killed my favorite cousin, and all fingers point to you." Toni said.

"Oh ok. We here, come on lets go take a look inside." Danni said getting out her car. Danni and Toni walked in the

215

house after Danni used the bottom of her shirt to open the unlocked door. When they walked in, she made sure not to touch anything. When she was walking to the stairs, she put on some latex gloves but Toni never saw her do it. They walked further in the house, a man grabbed Toni.

"What the fuck?" Toni said.

"Shut the fuck up bitch." The guy said.

The guy took Toni in the living room and sat her down in a chair. He tied her hands and feet to the chair and placed a gag in her mouth. He also checked her for wires or any weapons just in case, but found none. Toni started to squirm in the seat, so Danni took the gag from her mouth briefly.

"What the fuck is going on Danni?" Toni asked scared.

"I'm going to tell you like this. I don't take threats lightly. You threatened me one to many times. You just wouldn't leave me alone. You and your little boyfriend fucked up. So you always wanted to know who killed your cousin. It was me. I couldn't stand his abusive ass. So I had to do what I had to do. Now since you want to be nosey and shit, it is your time to go." Danni said.

"Wait Danni, I have a baby on the way, I have children. I only did it because he made me do it. Matter of fact he was following us the whole time so he will be busting in here in any minute now." Toni said with a smile.

As soon as Toni said that the back door of the house opened and Moe and Officer Jones walked in. Moe had a gun to Officer Jones head.

"Hey baby. I see you got our surprise guest." Danni said.

"You know I do ma." Moe said giving Danni a kiss after he pushed the officer towards Toni.

"You both are going to jail for life. I'll make sure of that." Officer Jones said.

"You won't have time to make sure we go to jail for life, because you'll be dead." Moe said shrugging.

"Oh, by the way Toni you aren't pregnant." Danni said with a smirk.

"What are you talking about?" Toni asked.

"You were never pregnant. I just needed to know what you wanted and why you kept coming around. It's called false positive bitch." Danni said.

"Yo, Killer we need to get this over with." The guy Kay said.

"Baby you ready to do this? We are running out of time." Moe asked Danni.

Danni nodded her head up and down. Moe passed her the gun with the silencer and he took one out of the bag of weapons. They took aim at their targets, knowing this would be the last time they would have to deal with them.

"Danni please I have children." Toni said crying hysterically.

"Your children would be better off without you." Danni said.

Danni looked at Moe and Moe looked at her. Then they both pulled the trigger, watching as their bullets penetrated their targets foreheads, killing them instantly.

"Give me the gun." Moe took the gun from her Danni.

"You did good lil momma." Kay said to Danni, tapping her shoulder.

"Thanks Kay. I'll see you at home babe." Danni said to Moe. Before Danni left, she gave Moe the cell phone and everything that he asked for. When she got in the car, she didn't cry or anything like she did the last time. She just drove home like it was nothing. When she got home she went straight to the shower. She was washing off, as Moe walked into the bathroom. He stripped and got in the shower behind her. They made love in the shower then went from the shower to the bedroom. He made sure that he made passionate love to Danni, as he went deeper and deeper in her tears rolled down Danni' cheeks. She held on to every word he said to her, the promises of loving her forever and the future that they would have.

"Damn you that were great baby." Danni said as she turned the TV on after they finished.

"Yeah, you just were turning me on when you shot that gun. Oh turn it to the news." Moe said.

As they watched the news, the reporter said *"There was a mass fire at an abandoned house on the 14th block of F Street. The victims are not identifiable and there are no suspects at this time. Stayed tuned for more coverage as it is made available."*

"I love you and I promise nothing will ever happen to you." Moe said kissing Danni's lips.

"I love you too. Thank you for being there for me." Danni said snuggling up to his chest. She knew that with this behind them, they would be able to move on and be at peace.

Chapter 38

Kim

Kim sat on the bed just looking in her closet trying to figure out what she wanted to put on. Today she and Quan were taking Xavier out for a family outing. She knew they were going go cart driving and skating, but she still didn't know what to put on.

"Damn baby you still in the same spot?" Quan said.

"Shut up, I don't know what I want to put on." Kim said.

"If you ain't have so many clothes that would be easy." Quan said.

"Whatever. What is your son doing?" Kim asked pulling at different shirts that were hanging up. Nothing was catching her eye.

"Watching cartoons dressed. Something your ass has to do." Quan said.

"Help me then, bae." Kim said pouting at him.

Quan went into Kim's closet, grabbed some jeans, a shirt and some Adidas.

"Now you done." Quan said handing her the clothes.

"Those jeans are too small and that shirt I wore when I was pregnant." Kim said looking at him with a raised eyebrow.

"Well, why you going to ask me to help you if you going to complain." Quan asked.

"I don't know. I just think it would be funny to see what you pick out. I'll be ready in 10 minutes." Kim said.

While Kim got ready, Quan went and had a business call. He talked to the caller and promised to meet up with them later. When he got off the phone, Kim was ready to go.

They went to the go carts first. Kim had a go cart by herself, while Quan shared with Xavier. They were having fun going around the track. As they finish go cart driving they went and got something to eat at *Friendly's* restaurant.

"So when are we going to increase the size of our family?" Quan asked.

"Whenever, I get a ring on this finger." Kim said immediately.

"Oh I got the ring. So when are we?" Quan asked.

"We can start whenever you want to." Kim said giving Quan the "it's whatever" look.

After they finished eating, they headed to the skating rink. Kim was a great skater, while Quan on the other hand couldn't even stand up on the skates. While Kim taught Xavier how to skate, Quan kicked his skates off and sat down.

"You quit fast babe." Kim said laughing.

"I can't do that shit. Those joints were hurting and everything." Quan said.

Kim was laughing so hard at Quan. She went back in the rink with X and while he skated forward she skated backwards. Enjoying their fun at the skating rink, they left.

"Daddy, can we go to the store?" Xavier said.

"Quan he don't need nothing else. He has been eating junk all day." Kim said.

"He alright, I got this." Quan said as he turned into the store parking lot.

Kim just shook her head. Quan went in the store and brought Xavier candy, chips, basically anything that was sweets. Xavier already had some candy and chips in the backseat so she knew he was going to be hyper as they came home.

"Don't you eat another piece of candy." Kim told him. She ran him some bath water and as soon as he was out the tub, he was still hyper and then he finally fell asleep.

"Quan, I'm going to kill you." Kim said to him when she walked into the room.

"What I do?" Quan asked.

"Because of you it took me a long time to get that boy to fall asleep because he was so hyper off that candy and stuff." Kim said.

"Well, come and kill me then." Quan said winking his eye at her.

Kim smiled and knew what he was talking about. She walked over to him and took his shirt off, kissing his chest, abs, neck, and lips. Then when she was about to go down on him, he stopped her.

"Baby you just relax this time. I'm going to take care of you."

Quan took his time with Kim. He made sure to please every inch of her body starting with slow kisses all over her body, moving down to her wet pussy lips. He wanted the night to be so special for her, so he gave her slow put powerful strokes with his tongue, while massaging her breast, after making her cum back to back he kissed up her body. Lingering on her lips he sucked her bottom lip, while entering her wet pussy. Feeling Kim's body melt into his, he took his time making love to her. Stroking and thrusting at a mind blowing force and pace. Kim felt like she was on a heavenly ride and didn't want him to stop. Holding on tightly they both didn't want this feeling to stop and felt as one at the moment.

"I love you." Quan said so passionately

"I love you too." Kim replied feeling in total bliss. Still holding tight to each other they both came long and hard.

He held her while she slept in his arms after they made love.

Quan was interrupted when his cell phone rang.

"Yeah?" Quan said. He listened to the caller, and then said "Give me 20 minutes." Getting out of the bed, he quickly took a shower and got re-dressed.

"Sunshine wake up." Quan said to Kim.

Kim opened up an eye and looked at him like he was crazy.

"Don't look at me like that girl… I got to tell you something." Quan said.

"Where are you going?" Kim asked.

"Well, I'm about to go meet these niggas about some business stuff. You know everything is in your name…"

"Why are you telling me all of this? You're going to be right back." Kim said, getting worried.

"I will be back but just in case. These some new cats, so you know the process. I love you sunshine."

"I love you too. Please don't go I have and bad feeling." Kim said sitting up, clinging to Quan's shirt.

"Everything is going to be iight." Quan said as he gave Kim a kiss.

She heard him go into Xavier's room and say something to him, then out the door he went.

Shawn…

"Who the hell is this calling me this time of night?" Shawn said out loud as he looked at his clock.

"Hello." Shawn said not looking at the caller id.

"Shawn, I have bad feeling, I didn't want him to leave. Go get him." Kim said crying hysterically.

"Kim? Why are you crying? Slow down so I can understand you." Shawn said.

"He went to meet somebody. I have a bad feeling. Go get him." Kim said slower.

"Did Quan say where he was going?" Shawn asked.

"No he just said these are some new cats. I don't feel right about this."

"Don't worry I'm going to go get him." Shawn said sitting up from his bed.

"Thank you so much, Shawn." Kim said still crying.

"It'll be alright baby girl." Shawn reassured her as he hung up the phone. Jumping out the bed, he grabbed some jeans, shirt, boots, and a gun. He called Quan's phone over and over but didn't get an answer, so he went to his guest room.

"Yo, Kevin get your ass up son, we got problems." Shawn said.

"What is it son?" Kevin asked sleepily.

"Call all of Q people." Shawn said.

Kevin had been staying with Shawn since he and India got into a fight. As Shawn asked, Kevin called all of Q people. They all were ready for war.

Shawn had called Quan again and he answered this time.

"Q, where the hell you at?" Shawn asked.

"I had to handle this business. I have a meeting with these new cats in Mo County."

"Yo, we on our way. Don't do shit till we get there." Shawn said.

"Yo, Shawn I'm good man, trust me." Quan said.

"I'm still on my way, love you bro."

"I'll be waiting for you. Love you too bro." Quan said hanging up.

Shawn knew something wasn't right. He had the feeling now.

"Yo Kev, let's get going." Shawn yelled running down the stairs.

Quan…

Quan got out the car and walked over to the warehouse. He made sure he had his gun on him and took a deep breath.

"What's up Smoke?" Quan said as he walked in the warehouse.

"Ain't shit Q. Ready to get this business done?" Smoke asked.

"You know it. So where you know these niggas from?"

"They were locked up with my cousin and he told me they good."

Quan walked in the warehouse and looked at the dude who sat behind the desk. He knew who the dude was when he saw him.

"Smoke, do you know these dudes?" Quan asked.

"This is my first time meeting them too, Q." Smoke said.

Quan looked the dude in the eye and said "What's up Reds."

"It's been a long time Q. It's funny we meeting like this." Reds said smirking.

"Yeah, so what can I do for you?" Quan asked taking a seat in the chair in front of the desk.

"First, you can let me know where your stash and shit is at, and then you can die." Reds said laughing.

"Well, you ain't getting shit from me and I think you'll be the one dying soon enough." Quan said leaning back in the chair.

"Oh Q you still the same hard ass nigga. I bet if I kill you and your whole little crew, or better yet how about I kill your girl and child."

"Fuck you dog. You ain't going to do shit you punk ass nigga."

"Poor poor Q, you thought the shooting at y'all little party was something. This time it won't be a warning."

"You still ain't getting shit." Quan said.

Reds looked around and laughed "This nigga thinks I'm playing with him."

Reds pulled his gun out and shot Smoke right in the head point blank range. When the bullet hit Smoke in the head Quan didn't move or anything.

"You next bitch or tell me where the shit at." Reds said angrily.

Quan just looked at him and pulled his cell phone out.

"Baby, where are you? Please come home." Kim said as soon as she picked up the phone.

Never taking his eyes off of Reds, Quan said "Look I need you to calm down. I'll be home soon, just have to wrap some shit up with some clown ass motherfucker. I wanted to call and tell you that I love you and when I get home we going to make it official we getting married tomorrow. Did you look at your left hand?"

Kim finally looked at her left hand and saw the most beautiful engagement ring. She didn't understand how she missed it.

"I love you too Quan and I can't wait to be your wife. I love the ring." Kim said crying.

"That's what's up. Put little man on the phone." Quan said.

"Hey daddy." Xavier said.

"Little man, take care of your mom. I love you." Quan said still having a staring contest with Reds.

"I am a big boy. I can take care of mommy. I love you too daddy." Xavier passed the phone to Kim.

"Iight baby girl I have to go." Quan said hanging up the phone before she could say something else.

"So you done Mr. Family man?" Reds asked.

"Fuck you dawg." Quan said.

"When I kill you, I'm going to love fucking that beautiful bitch of yours." Reds said laughing.

Quan was pissed now. He was ready to kill. He looked around and noticed he was outnumbered. He didn't care. He wasn't going out without a fight.

"Man fuck you." Quan said pulling out his guns. He started shooting, ducking and going towards his car. He was not going out like a punk. He had a mission and his mission was to make it back home to Kim.

Chapter 39

The Hospital

"Man I hope we ain't too late." Shawn said as the guys pulled up to the warehouse and got out the car.

"Yeah, me too son. Terence do you see him over there?" Moe asked.

They were walking around the warehouse with guns raised. They saw Quan's car so they knew he was in there.

"Yo Q." BJ yelled.

"Yo, come here?" Zoe said.

All of the dudes went to over to where Zoe was and shook their head.

"Damn they killed Smoke." Terence said.

"What the fuck was Quan doing with Smoke?" BJ asked.

Shawn had walked away from the group, still looking for his brother when he spotted another body. "Oh shit." He yelled. Falling down to the body on the ground, he checked for any sign of life.

All of the dudes heard him and went over to where he held Quan on his lap.

"Come on Quan. Say something." Shawn said, with tears rolling down his face.

"All I need is a name and they are dead I swear to God." Moe said.

Quan coughed up some blood and opened his eyes. He was weak. He had been shot numerous times.

"Reds." Quan said weakly. He was losing a lot of blood from the gun wounds.

"Hold on bro, I am going to get you to a hospital. Yo, help me get him up." Shawn said.

The guys picked him up and led him to Shawn truck. Kevin drove the truck, while BJ took Quan car. They were speeding to the hospital.

"Shawn… take care of Kim… treat her right." Quan said weakly.

"I won't have to man. You are going to make it and you going to take good care of her. Stop talking like this is the end." Shawn said with tears rolling down his face.

"Yo, call her. I have to hear her voice." Quan said.

Shawn pulled out his cell phone and called Kim like Quan asked.

"Shawn please tell me that you found him." Kim said as soon as she picked the phone up.

"Hey baby… I'm fine." Quan said taking deep breaths.

"You don't sound fine. Please tell me you coming home." Kim cried.

"Stop the crying…I have to get a band- aid then I'll be home…be strong and you know I love you" Quan said.

"I'm trying to be and I love you too. Shawn what hospital are y'all going to?" Kim asked hurriedly.

"Holy Cross. We have to go." Shawn hung up the phone.

Kim...

Kim got out the bed so fast that she almost fell. She picked up her phone and dialed her friend's number.

"India please get everyone to meet me at holy cross hospital." Kim said putting on her sweat pants and tennis shoes.

"What is going on Kim? Why are you crying? "India asked getting nervous.

"Something happened to Quan. I have to go." Kim said hanging up.

Kim picked Xavier up and ran out the door and hopped in the car.

When India got off the phone with Kim, she called all the girls and told them what to do.

When Kim got into the ER she went to the front desk and said "I'm looking for Quan Brown."

"Kim." She heard her name. She turned around and saw Shawn. She ran to him and hugged him so tight.

"Please tell me he is ok?" Kim said with tears streaming down her face.

"To be honest I don't know Kim. He lost a lot of blood." Shawn said.

Kim started to cry harder. He hugged her so she can cry on him and picked Xavier up and led her to where they were sitting.

They waited in the waiting room so long. Kim had fallen asleep on the chairs with Xavier in her arms.

"Are you ok sweetie?" Lisa asked as she walked over to Kim with the rest of the girls in tow.

Kim opened her eyes and saw her girls standing in front of her.

"Hey y'all." Kim said.

"So what did they say?" India asked.

"I haven't heard anything yet, but I think y'all need to talk to y'all boyfriends since we all here together." Kim said.

"Kim this is not the time or place. So it'll happen soon or later." London said.

As soon as London said that the doctor walked out and said "I'm looking for the immediate family of Quan Brown."

Everybody stood up and gave the doctor their full attention. All of Quan's friends and mother were there now.

"Well, he was shot several times. A bullet hit him in the chest and a bullet hit his lung. We tried to do everything, but we couldn't save him. I am so sorry." The doctor said.

Kim was stuck in place and started to shake. She fell to the floor crying and screaming. Shawn held her as tears ran down his face. There was no dry face in the waiting room. Terence comforted Quan's mother as she cried into his chest.

233

"Can I see him?" Kim asked.

"Only immediate family can come in the back." The doctor said.

"This is his wife. They all are his brothers". Quan's mother spoke up through her tears.

"Ok ma'am." The doctor said.

Shawn, Kim, Terence and Quan's mother went to the back. Moe, BJ, Zoe, Rico or Kevin couldn't see Quan like that. All they worried about was killing the person who did it.

The doctor pulled the blanket back enough so they could see his face. Shawn tried to stay strong but the more he looked at his brother's face the madder he got.

"Terence please escort me out of here." Quan's mother said as she let her tears fall.

"No problem ma." Terence looked over at Quan's body and said "I love you man, this ain't over."

Terence and Quan's mother left. Kim walked over to Quan's body and touched his face.

"Why you have to go? Please come back to me. Wake up Quan, please wake up. Don't leave me, I need you, Xavier needs you. Please, please just tell me this is a joke." Kim said crying so hard.

Shawn just stood back and watched Kim talk to Quan's lifeless body.

Kim kissed his lips, over and over as if he was sleep and her lips would wake him up. "I love you Quan, We were going to get married. PLEASE COME BACK TO ME!"

"Kim we have to go." Shawn walked over and put his hand over Kim's.

"Shawn bring him back. You just don't know how much I love him." Kim said falling into Shawn arms.

He picked her up, and looked at his brother one last time and said "I love you Quan, and I'll keep the promise."

Shawn drove Kim and Xavier home. After she had left the back from seeing Quan one last time she was in shock and didn't talk to anyone. She just sat there while her friends hugged her good-bye, telling her to get some rest. Shawn promised them that he would take care of her. Quan's mother was going through it too, but she knew she had to be strong, so she told Shawn she would come over and talk to Kim the next day.

Chapter 40

Let's Make up

Lisa...

"Ma, ever since this happened to Quan, I've been missing Terence a lot." Lisa said while she talked to her mother in the kitchen.

"I know baby. How is Kim doing?" Tonya said.

"She is trying to stay strong, but you can tell she hurting. I talked to her and she told me life is too short to be mad at each other."

"She is right. Go and get your man." Tonya told her daughter.

Lisa went upstairs and put on some clothes then left out the house. She drove to her house and she saw Terence's car in the driveway. She walked to the door and used her key. When the door opened, she heard him in the kitchen talking on the phone so she walked towards his voice.

"So who you talking to?" Lisa asked when she saw him standing in the kitchen with boxers on and the phone to his ear.

"Yo, I'm going to call you back." Terence said to the caller. He just looked at Lisa. "So what do I owe this visit?"

"I wanted to apologize for leaving the way that I did. I know that you just not going to take me back this easily. But I want you to know that I love you and I never stopped loving you. I just let my emotions get the best of me and I want you to take me back. Lisa said with tears in her eyes.

There was a silence between the both of them. Lisa took the no response and silence that he wanted her to leave so she turned around and started to walk out the door.

"Lisa." Terence said.

Lisa stopped walking and turned around to face him.

"You hurt me when you left, but I understand what you were saying. You don't have to worry about wanting me back, because you never lost me. I love you too ma." Terence said smiling.

Lisa ran and jumped in her man's arm. She showered him with kisses.

"Where is my little man?" Terence asked.

"He is with Larry. Now let's make up before we go get him." Lisa said, rubbing her hand up and down the front of his boxers, feeling him get hard.

Terence and Lisa had sex all over the house. They were like two teenagers who discovered what it felt like for the first time. When they were done, Terence got dressed and they went to Lisa's old house and got their son and Lisa and TJ belongings.

Tracey...

Tracey was getting ready to leave out the house. She was tired of being in the house packing. She had postponed her moving to California a week because she had to be there for Kim and her loss. Zoe hadn't been in the house for a week straight and Tracey really didn't care.

"Handsome come on. We about to go see your grandfather." Tracey said.

As they opened the door to leave out, Zoe was at the door.

"Damn, where you headed to?" Zoe asked.

"Out. Long time no see or hear." Tracey said.

"I know. I just been busy with a lot of stuff. I need to talk to you anyway, so I'm glad I caught you." Zoe said.

"Well, what you have to talk about?"

"Damn, can I come in to my house?" Zoe asked.

"It's a nice day, let's chill outside." Tracey said.

Tracey and Zoe sat outside on the step while Handsome played in the front yard.

"Well, I know I haven't been around, but I had to do some important business."

"So your business is more important than talking about my move?" Tracey asked cutting him off.

"No it's not. Can you just listen? I had to do this business so I can be able to move to San Diego next week with my family." Zoe said.

Tracey looked at him with wide eyes and smiled "You going to move with me?"

"That's what I said." Zoe replied.

Tracey immediately pulled him in for a hug and lingering kiss. Feeling on his chest when she pulled away, Zoe knew what it would lead to.

"Yo, lil man, come inside and watch some cartoons right quick while mommy and daddy talk." Zoe said grabbing Tracey's hand and smacking her ass with the other. Handsome sat on the floor, engrossed in SpongeBob square pants, while his parents went upstairs to "reconcile".

London…

It was a nice day outside, so London felt like putting some steaks and ribs on the grill. She made some pasta salad, and corn with her grilled food. While she was in the middle of cooking, she heard her door bell.

"Who is it?" London said.

"Open this door. I have to pee." Kim said.

London opened the door, and gave Kim, India, the twins, and Xavier a hug. Kim ran to the bathroom.

"What do I owe this visit?" London asked.

"Girl, I was over Kim house and she was like she wanted to get out of the house." India said.

"What's wrong? Is everything ok?" London asked.

"What? I just can't want to get out the house?" Kim asked as she walked in the kitchen from the bathroom.

"You can get out the house honey. You just ain't been wanting to lately." London said.

"Yeah, I know. What are you cooking? It smells good. I'm hungry." Kim said.

"Bitch you just ate. Is there something you want to tell us?" India asked.

"Bitch, I been depressed and haven't been eating." Kim said.

"Y'all dumb. Let's go out back." London said. They all went out back and watched the children run around playing while they had girl talk.

"So, London did you talk to BJ?" India asked.

"Have you talked to Kevin?" London asked.

"Fuck no. I can fuck his cousin up right now." India said.

"Yeah I feel you. He just mad because he gave up all his money and ain't get the right pussy." London said laughing.

"If you call BJ, I'll call Kevin." India said.

"Oh you don't have to call Kevin. He on his way over here with Shawn, you know that nigga always have to be where I'm at. It's getting on my nerves." Kim said.

"Well you have to call BJ chick." India said.

London picked up her cell phone and dialed his number.

"Hello." A female voice came through his phone.

240

"Umm may I speak with Brandon?" London said her heart in her stomach. She could hear the girl calling BJ's name.

"Hello." BJ said smoothly when he got on the phone.

"Hey, how you doing?" London said not sure what to say.

"I have been iight. What's up?" BJ asked not in the mood for small talk.

"So was that your new girl that answered your phone?" London couldn't help but ask, jealousy leaking from her voice.

"It's none of your business. What is your purpose for calling?" BJ asked trying to get straight to the point.

"I wanted to let you know that I was being selfish and I wanted to let you know that I'm keeping the baby." London said.

"Oh that's good. Talk to you later." BJ said.

"So all you have to say is that is good. I apologize and all you can say is that you'll talk to me later." London said.

"London just because you call and tell me this doesn't mean I'm going to run back to you. My got damn best friend was just murdered. You are right you are selfish. Like I said, I 'll talk to you later." BJ said.

"I'm sorry BJ. I want to be there for you but just because you angry for what happened we still have to live our life. I love you and I'm going to be here for you regardless." London said.

241

"You just don't know how it feels to have your best friend taken away from you. Then I had to worry about you killing my seed. This was a lot for someone to take."

"I know and I'm so sorry. Please come home tonight." London said.

"I will, but I really have to go." BJ said.

"So you have to get back to your new girlfriend?" London asked.

"There you go. I'm at Quan's mother house and that was his 15 year old cousin. I asked her to answer my phone for me. Oh and tell Kim she know her ass supposed to be over here." BJ said.

"Oh ok." London said, calming her anger some. "I'll see you tonight."

When she hung up she was smiling so hard.

"So I take it that that the conversation went well." India said.

"Hell yeah, he just been going through a lot. Oh and he said you know you supposed to be over Quan's mother house now." London said to Kim.

"I know but I didn't feel like being around all them. They make me depressed even more. Crying and all of that, I just don't want to be around that. His family came over and they talked and talked. They are begging for his shit." Kim said.

"Damn already. He hasn't even been gone for a whole week." London said.

242

"I know, I told them they can't have shit." Kim said.

India…

As India sat in London's house eating the food that London cooked on the grill, they were having the time of their lives going through memory lane. While they were talking, laughing, and eating they heard voices and right off the back India knew who it was.

"Hey ladies." Shawn said when he came through the backyard gate.

All the girls greeted Shawn.

"So what y'all over here doing? Talking about y'all hoeing days?" Kevin said.

"Yep, we were talking about how we use to get our back blown out and fucking any dude with a dick." India said sarcastically.

"Yeah, so how is your single life?" Kevin asked.

"Couldn't be better, I just met a politician. He is so sexy and stacked with the dough. He has lot of condos and don't mine moving me and my children in one." India said lying her ass off.

"Oh really? Does he know you ain't anything but a hoe?" Kevin asked angrily.

"The things I do for him in the bed he don't care what I was or am." India said.

"Man, I should just fuck your face up." Kevin said moving towards her.

"You are not going to do shit, Mr. Kevin." India said.

"Yo, Kev, calm down, you tripping. You told her to go ahead and live her life. Did you ever think about hearing your woman out?" Shawn asked because he knew Kevin should have listened to India from jump.

"You right dog. I was stupid taking my cousin side without hearing your side, but you know I get jealous when I hear niggas talking about they been with you or anything. So right here right now, tell me what happened." Kevin said

"You should have done that in the first place." Kim said ready to smack Kevin.

"Kim I got this." India said getting ready to tell him what happened. "Well, London had an internship in New York, so we thought it would be cool if all of us can hang in New York for a week. When we got there we partied since we were in college. So the last night we went to a club. In the club we had dudes trying to get at us everywhere. So this one crew, which your cousin was a part of, came to us off some trick stuff. Your cousin and his friends started to flash money and talking about they got our drinks, and was going to take us out. We didn't like how they were just throwing money at us, so we figured we would play them. So while we danced with them we dug in their pockets. Each of us made at least a thousand off of one of his friends not including the drinks they were buying us. So when the club was about to close, them niggas told us since they brought us drinks and stuff we had to meet them at Grand Hyatt hotel. They gave us room keys and everything. So we told them we need more money so on top of the thousand that we took, they gave us five hundred. So we knew they wasn't going to see us again, but to take it further, because they were acting like we were hoes, we got some prostitutes and gave them three hundred dollars, with the room number and key. We told them to keep the light off and that the dudes they were about to fuck were paid and where their money was. So they hopped on it and that is what happened." India said finishing her story.

"Yo, we got their asses good." London said laughing hard.

"Hell yeah." Kim said high fiving her.

The girls were laughing because they remembered the night clear as day.

"Are you serious?" Kevin asked with a stuck face.

"Yeah, you know I don't like to lie. I always told you the truth so why would I start lying now?" India asked.

"Son, she is right. You know India always kept it 100." Shawn said.

"Yeah, I know. I'm sorry baby, I was just angry that night. I just heard one side and I was stupid. So are you going to leave your politician alone and stay with a sad drug dealer?" Kevin asked grabbing her hand.

"Please say yes. I need my house back. Plus this nigga always crying talking about when is she going to call and shit." Shawn said.

"Shut the fuck up, ain't nobody been crying." Kevin said giving Shawn a death glare. "So what's it going to be?"

"When you put it that way, I guess I would have to stay with the sad drug dealer." India said laughing.

"Oh yeah, ay yo kids, daddy is back." Kevin said, turning to pick up his kids. When he put the twins down, he turned to India and gave her a wink. Pulling her to him, they got in a lip lock. Forgetting that they had an audience, India stated to reach for Kevin's belt buckle while he palmed her butt with both hands, in the process of picking her up. Common sense came back and India immediately let go of Kevin, excusing herself.

"I have to use the bathroom." India said breaking loose. She walked towards the back door and slipped inside, leaving it open.

"Yeah, me too." Kevin said walking towards the backdoor as well.

They went in the house but before they could get all the way in, London said "Don't fuck in my bathroom. If you do the cleaning stuff is under the counter."

Kim...

"Thanks Shawn, but you didn't have to carry him in the house. I had him." Kim said as she went into the house.

"Girl, stop being silly. This is my son." Shawn said as he took a sleeping Xavier upstairs.

"I know he's your son, but you just been doing a lot. Oh, take off his clothes. He has been playing all day in those." Kim said.

"First, you give me hell for carrying him in the house, now you giving me orders." Shawn said.

Kim just looked at him and left out of Xavier's room. Ever since Quan had got murdered she hasn't been in the house by herself, either one of her or Quan's friends were over, or his or her family member. She really hasn't had time to be alone and think. The way she was coping with it is thinking that he went out and would be back later.

"What are you thinking about?" Shawn asked as he walked in Kim's room and saw her just sitting there with a blank look.

Startled from her thoughts, she replied, "Oh nothing. Did you put his night clothes on?"

"Yeah, I did." Shawn said.

"Thank you Shawn, you don't have to stay the night." Kim told him.

"You sure?" Shawn didn't want her to be alone with their son in the house.

"Yes I'm positive. I have a lot to do tomorrow. I have to make sure they have the right outfit and everything together for the funeral." Kim said.

"Ok, before I leave I have to talk to you about something." Shawn said.

"Ok go head I'm listening." Kim said.

"Well, I want to tell you I love you, you are the woman I wanted to be with my whole life. If I can't have you, I don't want anyone else. I made a promise to my brother that I would take care of you and make sure you would be happy. This is something I wanted to do for years but was always scared to do it. Kimberly Williams will you marry me?" Shawn asked getting down on one knee.

"What? You have to be kidding me." Kim said starting to cry.

"I love you and want to be with you the rest of my life." Shawn said.

Kim got up and ran to the bathroom and locked the door.

"Kim open the door." Shawn said banging on it.

"He hasn't even been gone a whole week. Why would you do this?" Kim said yelling. Kim was crying and her stomach started to get weak. She crawled to the toilet and started throwing up.

"Kim are you ok in there?" Shawn asked.

"Just leave, get out." Kim yelled.

When she thought Shawn was gone, she curled up in the floor and cried and talked to Quan's spirit.

"Why you leave me? I need you, come back. I really need you to hold me now." Kim said rocking gently on the floor looking at the ring Quan had gave her.

As she dozed off on the floor her cell phone rung in her back pocket.

"Hello." Kim said still sounding like she was crying.

"Are you ok?" Danni asked.

"No, I need to talk to you. I'll come pass tomorrow after I finish doing all the arrangements." Kim said.

"Ok, whatever you need hun." Danni said.

Chapter 41

The Funeral (Shawn)

"I can't believe I'm going to my brother's funeral."
Shawn said out loud as he drove to Kim's house to meet
everybody. When he pulled up, everybody was outside by the
limousines, and cars were everywhere. Quan knew a lot of
people and family was everywhere.

"What's up Shawn?" BJ said.

"Nothing man. Trying to stay strong." Shawn said.

"Yeah, I feel you." BJ said.

Shawn walked over to Kim's family.

"Hey, ma. What's up Angel pies?" Shawn said talking to
Kim's mother and sister.

"Just trying to make sure my daughter is going to be ok."
Mia said.

"Me too." Shawn said. "Me too."

While Shawn was talking to Kim's family, he heard a
man call his name.

"Hey boy." Shawn turned to the voice and saw his
father.

"What are you doing here?" Shawn asked.

Shawn and Quan were a mixture of their father. He was
Carmel, with light brown eyes, waves in his hair and nice lips.

"That was my son." Capone said. Capone was a name that he earned off the street back in his hay day.

"If it wasn't for you, he would still be here, and our life wouldn't be so fucked up." Shawn said pissed off.

"Who you talking to like that?" Capone asked stepping up to Shawn.

"I'm talking to you. Fuck you. I am going to make sure that my son doesn't end up like we did." Shawn said. Shawn couldn't stand being around his father. As he walked off, Capone just stood and looked at his son, as he picked Xavier up.

"Xavier where is your mom?" Shawn asked.

"In the room. She crying." Xavier said.

Shawn put him down and ran upstairs. When he got upstairs, she was laying across her bed with the trash can next to her, tissues all over the bed, and her girls standing around.

"What is wrong, with her?" Shawn asked.

"She not feeling well and she don't want to go." Lorren said.

"Yo, let me talk to Kim alone right quick. Tell them we will be ready to go in 15 minutes." Shawn said.

All the girls cleared the room.

"Kim, come on you have to be strong. If you could give me one reason why you shouldn't go, I will go downstairs and let everyone know you not going." Shawn said.

"I'm hurting Shawn. I was so in love with him it was crazy. I can't see him like that. I want to just remember him the way he was. And to top it off I'm pregnant." Kim said blowing her nose.

Shawn went over to her and put her on his lap. He held her and rocked her while she cried.

"Quan wouldn't want you to be depressed. He would want you to be there. The baby issue, that's nothing. He took care of you when you were pregnant with my child and I will do the same. I will raise him as if he is my own. Me and you made a promise to Quan before he died. I promise to keep you happy and safe, and you promise to be strong for him. So are you going to go?" Shawn asked wiping tears from her face.

"Yes, I'm going to get dressed." Kim said.

Shawn left the room and let Kim get dressed. He made sure everything was in order and within 15 minutes, he had everybody in the cars headed to the church. When they got to the church people were crying everywhere. The singing and preaching had people crying. When it was time for Kim to go up and talk about Quan she couldn't, she tried but she was crying to bad. All of Quan's friends said something in his respect. When it was the time to view the body one last time, Shawn helped Kim.

"Kim are you ok?" Shawn asked.

"Yes, I just want to see him." Shawn walked her up to the casket and Kim said she loved him and kissed him on the lips. Then she put a picture of him, her and Xavier in with him.

252

"Come on Kim." Shawn said. When he looked up and in the back of the church he saw the person he could have killed right there, "Reds".

Reds looked at him and did his hand like a gun and pointed to Shawn.

If you're interested in becoming an author for True Glory Publications, please submit three, completed chapters of your manuscript to Trueglorypublications@gmail.com.

Thank you for your interest!

Here is a list of other links that have been released by True Gory Publications:

Tiffany Stephens

Expect the Unexpected Part 1

http://www.amazon.com/Expect-Unexpected-Tiffany-Stephens-ebook/dp/B00J84URUM/ref=sr_1_1?ie=UTF8&qid=1413570346&sr=8-1&keywords=TIFFANY+STEPHENS

Expect the Unexpected Part 2

http://www.amazon.com/Expect-Unexpected-2-Tiffany-Stephens-ebook/dp/B00LHCCYG8/ref=sr_1_2?ie=UTF8&qid=1413570346&sr=8-2&keywords=TIFFANY+STEPHENS

Kim Morris: Tears I Shed Part 1 & 2

http://www.amazon.com/Tears-I-Shed-Kim-Morris/dp/1499319800

http://www.amazon.com/Tears-I-Shed-2-
ebook/dp/B00N4FD03C

Sha Cole

Her Mother's Love Part 1

http://www.amazon.com/Her-Mothers-love-Sha-Cole-
ebook/dp/B00H93Z03I/ref=sr_1_1?s=digital-
text&ie=UTF8&qid=1405463882&sr=1-
1&keywords=her+mothers+love

Her Mother's Love Part 2

http://www.amazon.com/HER-MOTHERS-LOVE-Sha-
Cole-
ebook/dp/B00IKBGWW6/ref=pd_sim_kstore_1?ie=UTF8
&refRID=1EFA9EPXRPBSQPZVWHM0

Her Mother's Love Part 3

http://www.amazon.com/Her-Mothers-Love-Sha-Cole-
ebook/dp/B00L2SHLNI/ref=pd_sim_kstore_1?ie=UTF8&r
efRID=1AW831PBNBGAPPP9G8A9

Guessing Game

http://www.amazon.com/Guessing-Game-Sha-Cole-ebook/dp/B00ODST1AA/ref=sr_1_8?ie=UTF8&qid=1413041318&sr=8-8&keywords=Sha+Cole

Niki Jilvontae

A Broken Girl's Journey

http://www.amazon.com/BROKEN-GIRLS-JOURNEY-Niki-Jilvontae-ebook/dp/B00IICJRQK/ref=sr_1_5?ie=UTF8&qid=1413419382&sr=8-5&keywords=niki+jilvontae

A Broken Girl's Journey 2

http://www.amazon.com/BROKEN-GIRLS-JOURNEY-ebook/dp/B00J9ZM9YW/ref=sr_1_4?ie=UTF8&qid=1413419382&sr=8-4&keywords=niki+jilvontae

A Broken Girl's Journey 3

http://www.amazon.com/BROKEN-GIRLS-JOURNEY-ebook/dp/B00JVDFTBM/ref=sr_1_1?ie=UTF8&qid=1413419382&sr=8-1&keywords=niki+jilvontae

A Broken Girl's Journey 4: Kylie's Song

http://www.amazon.com/Broken-Girls-Journey-Kylies-Song-

ebook/dp/B00NK89604/ref=sr_1_6?ie=UTF8&qid=14134
19382&sr=8-6&keywords=niki+jilvontae

A Long Way from Home

http://www.amazon.com/Long-Way-Home-Niki-Jilvontae-
ebook/dp/B00LCN252U/ref=sr_1_3?ie=UTF8&qid=14134
19382&sr=8-3&keywords=niki+jilvontae

Your Husband, My Man Part 2 KC Blaze

http://www.amazon.com/Your-Husband-Man-YOUR-

HUSBAND-

ebook/dp/B00MUAKRPQ/ref=sr_1_1?ie=UTF8&qid=141

3593158&sr=8-1&keywords=your+husband+my+man+2

Your Husband, My Man Part 3 KC Blaze

http://www.amazon.com/Your-Husband-My-Man-3-

ebook/dp/B00OJODI8Y/ref=sr_1_1?ie=UTF8&qid=14135

93252&sr=8-

1&keywords=your+husband+my+man+3+kc+blaze

Child of a Crackhead I Shameek Speight

http://www.amazon.com/CHILD-CRACKHEAD-Part-1-

ebook/dp/B0049U4W56/ref=sr_1_1?s=digital-

text&ie=UTF8&qid=1413594876&sr=1-

1&keywords=child+of+a+crackhead

Child of a Crackhead II Shameek Speight

http://www.amazon.com/CHILD-CRACKHEAD-II-

Shameek-Speight-

ebook/dp/B004MME12K/ref=sr_1_2?ie=UTF8&qid=1413

593375&sr=8-2&keywords=child+of+a+crackhead+series

Pleasure of Pain Part 1 Shameek Speight

http://www.amazon.com/Pleasure-pain-Shameek-Speight-ebook/dp/B005C68BE4/ref=sr_1_1?s=digital-text&ie=UTF8&qid=1413593888&sr=1-1&keywords=pleasure+of+pain

Infidelity at its Finest Part 1 Kylar Bradshaw

http://www.amazon.com/INFIDELITY-AT-ITS-FINEST-Book-ebook/dp/B00HV539A0/ref=sr_1_sc_1?s=digital-text&ie=UTF8&qid=1413595045&sr=1-1-spell&keywords=Infideltiy+at+its+finest

Infidelity at its Finest Part 2 Kylar Bradshaw

http://www.amazon.com/Infidelity-Finest-Part-Kylar-Bradshaw-ebook/dp/B00IORHGNA/ref=sr_1_2?s=digital-text&ie=UTF8&qid=1413593700&sr=1-2&keywords=infidelity+at+its+finest

Marques Lewis

It's Love For Her part 1 http://www.amazon.com/Its-Love-Her-Marques-Lewis-ebook/dp/B00KAQAI1A/ref=la_B00B0GACDI_1_3?s=books&ie=UTF8&qid=1413647892&sr=1-3

It's Love For Her 2 http://www.amazon.com/Its-Love-For-Her-ebook/dp/B00KXLGG5O/ref=pd_sim_b_1?ie=UTF8&refRID=1ABE9DSRTHFFH13WGH6E

It's Love For Her 3 http://www.amazon.com/Its-Love-For-Her-ebook/dp/B00NUOIP0A/ref=pd_sim_kstore_1?ie=UTF8&refRID=1PYKVRTJJJMYCHE0P5RQ

Words of Wetness http://www.amazon.com/Words-Wetness-Marques-Lewis-ebook/dp/B00MMQT2OU/ref=pd_sim_kstore_2?ie=UTF8&refRID=1FJFWTZSN2DBCV6PX3MG

He Loves Me to Death Sonovia Alexander

http://www.amazon.com/HE-LOVES-DEATH-LOVE-Book-ebook/dp/B00I2E1ARI/ref=sr_1_1?s=books&ie=UTF8&qid=1416789703&sr=1-1&keywords=sonovia+alexander

Silent Cries Sonovia Alexander

http://www.amazon.com/Silent-Cries-Sonovia-Alexander-ebook/dp/B00FANSOEQ/ref=sr_1_6?s=books&ie=UTF8&qid=1416789941&sr=1-6&keywords=sonovia+alexander+silent+cries

Ghetto Love Sonovia Alexander

http://www.amazon.com/GHETTO-LOVE-Sonovia-Alexander-ebook/dp/B00GK5AP5O/ref=sr_1_5?s=books&ie=UTF8&qid=1416790164&sr=1-5&keywords=sonovia+alexander+ghetto+love

Robert Cost

Every Bullet Gotta Name Part 1

http://www.amazon.com/dp/B00SU7KJ7O

Every Bullet Gotta Name Part 2

261

http://www.amazon.com/dp/B00TE7PSGG

Made in the USA
San Bernardino, CA
06 January 2016

3 1143 00929 7913